SHELF NINE

HAPPILY

EVER AFTER

Lisa Yarost

ISBN: 979-8-9919453

ISBN-13: 979-8-9919453-3-2

In memory of

my mother,

Sharon Klynstra.

You were the first person
to teach me about love.

ACKNOWLEDGMENTS

Thanks to my husband and to Emma Montgomery, who kept me motivated by alpha reading each scene as it came hot off the keyboard.

Thanks to Julie Hedden, whose fearless critique helped my book become its best.

And thanks to my readers for choosing to spend their time in Huntsville, Alabama, with Alison and Jack.

All of you help to make my dreams come true.

CONTENTS

CHAPTER ONE

Yours Truly

Tuesday, January 3

Alison

Alison slipped her final love letter into its acrylic holder and set it on the pink display table near the front of Happily Ever After Books. This one—addressed to Mr. Darcy—was her favorite, highlighting his quiet generosity and devotion.

A dozen letters were scattered throughout the shop, each numbered for her customers to guess the intended recipient. It was Alison's first promotional event of the year, and the winner of her "Yours Truly" contest would earn a gift certificate.

Bella, her black-and-white Shih Tzu, impatiently whined at her feet.

"Okay, Bella Baby, time to go."

Alison gathered her purse, snapped on Bella's leash, and switched off the fairy lights twinkling across the shelves. Beyond the windows, the lights of Huntsville, Alabama glowed in the winter's early darkness.

By 7 pm, Lowe Mill had gone still, its hallways hushed but for Alison and Bella's footsteps. A flash of fur—a mill cat—vanished into the shadows. Bella bristled but stayed at her side. The stairwell reeked of ammonia from the bats hidden in the rafters, and Alison breathed a sigh of relief when they stepped into the crisp January night.

She opened the backseat door with a "Hup!" and Bella bounded inside. Alison buckled in and started the car.

Then, her phone pinged.

> **Quinn:** Ali, how have you been?
> **Alison:** Fine. What do you want?
> **Quinn:** Don't be that way. You've been on my mind lately. Thought we might catch up. Coffee tonight? Bart's & Global?
> **Alison:** Seriously? You want me to drink coffee at a chain bookstore? Do you not remember how I make my living?
> **Quinn:** Sorry. Just trying to find somewhere close to you. How about City Cafe, 8:30?

Alison stared at the screen, lips pressed thin. Months without a word, and suddenly she was on his mind? *Please.* With a sigh, she typed her reply.

> **Alison:** OK
> **Quinn:** Can't wait

She hadn't forgotten who he was—or what he'd done.

Her mother's voice echoed in her head: *Once a cheater, always a cheater.*

So why go? Curiosity, nothing more. Alison had no desire to rekindle anything. What she wanted was groveling—his apology, his regret—so she could shove it back in his smug face. She pictured Quinn with his stupid, handsome eyes brimming with tears, begging. The image filled her with enough satisfaction to make her almost buoyant as she drove Bella home past the restaurant she and Quinn had once frequented and through her quiet neighborhood lined with tidy cottages.

At her mailbox, she retrieved the day's envelopes, checked her Little Free Library, and headed back inside. Determined to look stunning when she rejected Quinn Walton, Alison brushed out her long brown hair and tied it back to show off the highlights. She freshened her makeup and dabbed on her favorite perfume, then admired her new glasses with a smile as she pushed them back into place.

Tonight, he'd remember exactly what he'd lost.

Alison

Alison purposely arrived at the City Cafe ten minutes late, only to find that Quinn still hadn't shown.

So much for him spotting me the moment I walked in.

She slid into a booth with red vinyl benches and ordered a slice of cake to take home for breakfast. Annoyed by Quinn's habitual disregard for her time, she added a coffee and told the server she was waiting for someone.

By the time Quinn strolled in — another ten minutes later — Alison had rehearsed several ways of ignoring him.

Unfortunately, he'd already caught her watching the door and answered with a dazzling grin.

Of course, he did.

Quinn moved with the same casual confidence as always, as if the world had laid out a welcome mat just for him. His dark, wavy hair fell in perfect disarray, his jaw shaded with two days' stubble. He shrugged off his expensive leather jacket and tossed it into the booth before sliding in across from her.

"Ali," he said, voice smooth as hot chocolate. "It's been too long."

Says you.

The young waiter hurried over, eager to pour Quinn's coffee, eager to impress. Alison pitied him.

Sweet child, don't waste your time. It would only end in tears.

"What do you want, Quinn?" she asked flatly.

His expression faltered, eyes wide and pleading. "I told you—I've been thinking a lot about you lately. I wanted to catch up. Why is that so hard to believe?"

Alison tipped sugar and two creamers into her cup and stirred hard enough to slosh coffee onto the saucer. "You didn't think about me when we lived in the same house. Why now?"

He tilted his gaze toward the ceiling and softened his voice for maximum effect. "My grandmother. She loved books, just like you. Treasured them."

"Mhm." Alison stacked her empty creamer cups, bracing herself.

"And she would have wanted her treasures to stay in the family," Quinn continued.

"Then you shouldn't have cheated on the person you gave her treasure to." She tapped the little cups against the table instead of throwing them at his infuriating face.

"I didn't know we'd be breaking up," he said.

She raised an eyebrow. "You assumed I'd stay after finding out you were sleeping with someone else?"

He ignored the question. "Anyway, to honor her memory, I should keep her special edition of *Pride and Prejudice* in the family."

"That ship's already sailed." Alison flagged down the waiter for her cake.

"Please, Alison," Quinn pressed. "My mother's upset that I let you keep Grandma's Peacock Edition. I need it back."

"Your mother was there when you gave it to me, and she was thrilled. The book is mine, Quinn—no matter how much you've since learned it's worth."

Alison slid out of the booth and pulled on her jacket.

"Wait—there was something else." His eyes softened into another puppy dog plea. It was nauseating to admit she had ever believed a word he said.

"What?" The word came out sounding more like a demand than a question. She buttoned her coat while she waited for the cake.

"I wanted to tell you before you heard from someone else." A pause, then: "I'm getting married."

For a moment, her hands stilled on her buttons as the words shattered her. She had wasted three years of her life with Quinn. He had hinted at marriage for the last six months of it, right up until she'd uncovered his cheating.

She no longer wanted Quinn. Of that, she was certain.

So why did her chest ache? Why did the question slip in uninvited?

Why wasn't I good enough?

"Congratulations," Alison said briskly. "I hope you don't cheat on her, too."

She grabbed her purse as the waiter reappeared with a slice of cake so large it nearly split the clamshell container. Alison took it in a shaking hand, left Quinn with the bill, and walked out before her tears betrayed her.

"I'll stop by the shop on Saturday to pick up the book," Quinn called after her.

She ignored him as she pushed into the chilly night.

Quinn Walton and his charming smile could go take a flying leap at the moon.

Alison

Alison shushed Bella's bark as she opened her cottage door, balancing the cake container.

"Baby Bella! Why are you such a noisy thing? I told you to be good while I was gone."

The Shih Tzu launched her stocky little body toward Alison in greeting, tail streaming.

"One more walk before bed?"

Bella answered with a playful growl and plopped down beneath the leash hook.

"All right, you." Alison set the cake on the entry table beside her purse and clipped Bella's pink leash onto her matching collar. "You're more trouble than you're worth."

Every moment with Bella was a balm to her bruised heart.

The wind had picked up outside, sharp despite the temperature lingering above freezing. Alison tugged her coat tighter. The dog pranced ahead, taking time to greet neighboring dogs on the way.

Back inside, Alison's glasses fogged in the warmth. Bitterness followed close behind, and she sighed as she dropped her keys on the entry table.

She pulled her beloved vintage edition of *Pride and Prejudice* from the shelf and curled up on the couch. She lingered over the teal leather cover with its gilded peacock design and admired the illustrations.

Quinn had given it to her on Valentine's Day. At the time, it had meant everything. Now he wanted it back, to gift to his fiancée, maybe, or to sell for wedding money. Either way, returning it would make her prized possession a wedding present for her cheating ex. His fiancée could have him, but Alison had earned the book by surviving the heartache he caused.

Alison set the book down and reached for the cake instead.

Just one bite.

Caramel, peanuts, frosting—bite after delicious bite disappeared. The sweet comfort did little to quiet the question looping through her mind: keep the book and punish Quinn, or give it back and never see his phony smile again?

Unable to decide, she reached for another distraction— her phone. Tuesday nights always brought her least favorite ritual: hate reading Jack Morrison's Love Is a Scam column.

With each forkful of cake, she read his tirade against Valentine's Day. She polished off both the Snickers cake and the column, chasing them with a glass of milk.

She set her fork aside, stomach heavy with regret.

Valentine's Day is six weeks away, for Pete's sake. I wish I could make my living complaining about holidays.

CHAPTER TWO

The Queen of England

Saturday, January 7

Alison

Alison tied a pink bow onto Bella's collar, readying her for the launch of Happily Ever After Books's "Yours Truly" promotion. Bella trotted behind her like a fluffy metronome, tail curled over her back, likely planning the best spots to become an instant tripping hazard.

Alison adjusted displays, taping down vases to keep the fresh flowers from toppling at the first brush of a purse. Their fragrance mingled with the new-book scent, filling the shop with an atmosphere something close to heaven. Later, she'd corral Bella into her makeshift office—just a desk and worktable fenced off with white bookcases and a swinging baby gate.

Her gaze kept snagging on the teal and gold spine of *Pride and Prejudice*. She'd placed it with the stack of online orders and "Blind Date with a Book" packages. No matter how busy she got, her eyes found it. Should she keep her treasure or surrender it to Quinn for peace of mind?

After tying on a vintage apron, she dumped a pile of golf pencils into a chipped butter dish beside stacks of contest entry forms. Morning light softened her pink walls to warm peach. She watered her philodendrons, emptied the extra water into Bella's dish, and shut the gate.

All the love letters stood aligned on their display tables. By 11 am, Lowe Mill was open. Alison dragged a heavy wooden sandwich board into the hall to catch cafe traffic, then returned to packing online orders in the quiet stretch before customers trickled in.

Bella's nails scrabbled against the gate, tail wagging at the sound of footsteps. Alison poked her head around a bookcase. A man wandered the store, coffee in hand, eyes sliding across her love letter displays with less interest than Bella gave them.

"I'll be right there!" she called.

"No hurry," he drawled.

Alison stepped around her dog and squeezed through the baby gate. The sight that met her was underwhelming: a tight smile that didn't reach golden-brown eyes, brown curls sticking out at odd angles, a jaw shadowed with sleepless stubble over skin so pale it probably hadn't seen daylight in months.

"Are you browsing for yourself today, or picking up a gift for someone special?" His rumpled shirt looked slept-in, as did his pants.

He scoffed, pulling a card from his pocket. "I'm looking for Alison Hughes."

She glanced down. The card read: JACK MORRISON, JOURNALIST, ALABAMA ONLINE.

Her pulse jumped. *Jack Morrison? Love Is a Scam Jack Morrison? You call yourself a journalist?*

"I'm Alison Hughes." She gave him her sweetest smile, feigning a second look at the card. "Jack, is it? What can I do for you?"

Alison

"Alabama Online would like to do a Valentine's Day profile on you and your...business." Jack said *business* like it had air quotes around it.

"How exciting," Alison gushed, masking the tension pulling at her shoulders. She could only imagine what Mr. Love Is a Scam would write about a romance bookstore. "Why don't you come back into my office where we can sit and talk? You're okay with dogs?"

I'll bet he hates animals, too.

"Dogs are fine. Friendly, right?" He eyed Bella as if she might lunge at his chinos.

"I wouldn't have her here otherwise. Try not to let her out."

As Alison stepped through the gate, Bella bolted past, bouncing up to greet her new "best friend." Jack bent instinctively to pet her.

So, at least he doesn't hate animals. Not pure evil.

"Bella, sit!" The dog ignored her and circled Jack, tail wagging like a feather duster gone rogue.

"She's more tail than dog," Jack muttered, setting his coffee down.

You're as funny in person as you are in your column.

Alison gave a bright, practiced laugh. "She adores the attention of being groomed. If she didn't, I'd keep her tail trimmed short. You can pet her, but I'll send her to her bed if you'd prefer."

"No, I'll say hi." Jack offered his hand. Bella sniffed, licked, and then rolled belly-up, demanding more.

"Don't fall for it," Alison warned.

His eyes met Alison's as his hand recoiled a few inches. "Why? Will she attack?"

"Nothing like that. But once you start, she'll expect belly rubs for the rest of the day."

Jack chuckled under his breath before his gaze drifted to the Peacock Edition sitting on the table. "You sell used books too?"

"That one isn't for sale. It's mine." Alison moved it further from the edge. "So, this profile. What does it involve?"

"The usual. I interview you, take some photos, then do a writeup. How long will the mystery letters stay up?"

"Just this week. You can play along, if you like."

As if you'd know anything about romance.

"Ha. No thanks. They're not bad, though. AI can do impressive work these days."

"AI?" Alison's pulse spiked. "You think my letters were written by a bot?" Heat rushed to her cheeks. "Is that how you crank out the same whining drivel every week? Let an algorithm spew carbon while you sit back and sneer at people with hearts?"

Jack's eyes narrowed. "I knew you recognized my name. You read every word I write, don't you?"

"Every word you *tell AI* to write," Alison shot back.

"I do not use AI. My columns make more sense than the drivel you peddle to lonely, deluded women. If anything deserves a feature in *Love Is a Scam*, it's a romance bookstore."

Her eye twitched. "If you've already decided what to write, you don't need me. You're welcome to leave."

"Gladly. I didn't want to waste my time on your silly pink shop and frilly grandma aprons anyway."

He shoved to his feet, jostling the table. His coffee tipped, spilling across Alison's precious book.

She froze as the stain spread like a wound across the pages.

Alison

"No!" Alison snatched the book from the table to blot the coffee away. The paper towel she grabbed was useless against the spreading stain. Tears stung her eyes. "You ruined it! This book survived 125 years, and you destroyed it in one careless moment."

"I'm sorry." Jack exhaled, hurried and shallow. "Let me pay you. What was it, seventy-five dollars?"

Her jaw dropped. "Seventy-five? Before you ruined it, this 1894 illustrated Peacock Edition of *Pride and Prejudice* was worth twenty-two hundred dollars. You're an idiot, Jack Morrison."

His eyes widened, then narrowed as his jaw clenched until a vein stood out at his temple. "You're inflating the price to milk me. That book can't be worth—"

Alison pulled the appraisal certificate from the book, coffee-stained at the edges but still legible. "Not everyone's out to rip you off. You just destroyed my favorite thing in the world...outside of Bella. Pay up."

Jack paled as he scanned the paper. His shoulders slumped. "I don't have the money," he mumbled.

"What? *What?*" Alison's head throbbed.

Now I can't have the book, and I couldn't return it to Quinn if I wanted to.

He cleared his throat as his eyes looked everywhere but at her. "I don't have twenty-two hundred dollars, Alison. I'm sorry. Could I pay installments? A hundred a month?"

People buy cars on shorter installment plans.

She slammed the book shut and flinched when the pages met with a wet slap. "No! I needed the book, or the money to replace it, not a trickle for the next two years."

"I'm broke," Jack said. "Is there anything else I can do to make it up to you?"

Alison looked out into the empty hallway of Lowe Mill and sighed. She swallowed her tears. "Fine. Here's what we'll do. Valentine's Day is in six weeks. I've scheduled a promotion each week leading up to it. If you help me run every event and top it off with a glowing profile of Happily Ever After Books, maybe the store will earn enough extra to cover the loss. Fail, and I'll see you in small claims court."

"You're threatening me?"

"I'm offering you a deal," she snapped. "Don't try to *scam* me, Jack."

"I don't take advantage of people," he shot back.

Right.

He huffed. "What do you want me to do first?"

"Next weekend is our couple's book club. You'll submit blurbs to the local event calendars and assist me in hosting Friday's event."

Jack shifted uncomfortably, glancing around at the pink walls. "Couple's book club? I'm not the first man to walk in here?"

Alison arched a brow. "Hardly, so suck it up, Buttercup. Until Valentine's Day, I'm your boss. Now go. I'm still too angry to look at you."

"Fine." His voice cut sharp, but he bent to scratch Bella behind the ears, anyway. She rolled happily onto her back, tail thumping. "See you later, Rag Mop."

"It's *Bella*," Alison barked. "I'll see you a week from Friday. And those blurbs had better be good—no AI nonsense."

"I don't use AI," Jack called over his shoulder with a dismissive wave. "I'm a journalist."

Alison glared at the ruined book in her hands.

And I'm the Queen of England.

Alison

Alison dabbed page after page with paper towels, fighting to salvage her ruined book. Each stained leaf felt like a fresh wound. At least Jack's coffee had been black. Cream and sugar would have been worse. Still, the coffee stains clung, impossible to erase.

Jack Morrison had decided the matter for her. The book was no longer fit to return to Quinn. Even knowing the spill was an accident, Alison couldn't shake her resentment.

I'll never forgive him. Why would I?

Finally, she set the book aside and forced her attention back to the store. Customers clustered around the "Yours Truly" displays, phones out as they scoured the Internet for answers. Alison smirked at their fruitless searches—she'd made sure the letters offered clues while giving nothing away.

At three o'clock, Monique Willis arrived with her typical confident stride, and relief washed over Alison. Monique's steady presence was the anchor her weekends needed. Most of Alison's part-timers were college students; energetic but inconsistent.

Monique, at forty-seven, brought maturity, patience, and two years of loyal service. The job funded Monique's growing romance collection, but to Alison, Monique provided something rarer: stability.

Spotting the ruined book drying on the desk, Monique winced. "Did you do that? I'd be sick."

Alison sighed. "Jack Morrison did. The columnist." She told Monique about the previous night.

"Quinn didn't deserve that book back anyway," Monique muttered.

"I wasn't giving it back because he deserved it," Alison said. "It would've bought me peace."

"You should've kept it as compensation for pain and suffering."

"I considered it. Now it's ruined, and I'm sad either way." Alison straightened pencils, then fussed with the display table as they spoke. "How was work last night?"

"Same as always. Lonely. Boring. Productive. Nobody grows up dreaming of dispatching trucks at 3 am." Monique's fingers trailed over the spines, looking for misplaced titles. "This weekend's promotion should be fun. Anyone guessed all twelve recipients yet?"

"Someone got nine."

Monique's brows arched. "Impressive."

"I thought so." Alison took a long sip from her massive travel mug, then froze, shoulders tight. "Ugh. Look who's coming."

Quinn swept in, crisp shirt and tie under his expensive leather jacket, flashing Monique a dazzling smile. She answered with a smirk as dry as dust.

"Ali, how are you today?" Quinn leaned against the bookcase Alison was dusting, striking a practiced pose.

"Fine. What can I do for you?"

"I'm here for *Pride and Prejudice*." His smile never faded.

"We have five different editions," Monique offered.

"Ali knows which one I want."

"Too bad. You're not getting it." Alison's feather duster never paused.

"Why would you want something that reminds you of your old boyfriend?"

"It doesn't remind me of you. It reminds me of your grandmother."

"You never even met my grandmother." His scowl deepened.

"That's why I like her more than you." Alison adjusted her glasses, tone even. "If you want a copy so badly, buy one online. This one's mine."

His eyes narrowed to steel. "I'll keep asking until you give it back."

"Go ahead, waste your time. Though I wonder—does your fiancée know how much time you spend chasing your ex? She might think you're cheating again."

Quinn's mouth opened, but more customers bustled in before he could speak. Alison slipped past him to greet them, wiping dust from her glasses with her apron.

Monique, still shelving, chirped brightly, "They're right here! You'd be supporting your local indie bookstore."

Quinn shot Alison a sharp side-eye, then stalked out, footsteps as crisp as his scowl.

CHAPTER THREE

The Belly of the Beast

Saturday, January 7

Jack

Jack pulled up to the access box at the wooden and steel gate to his apartment complex. The heavy gate rolled open with a low groan after he inserted his key card, revealing several single-story apartment buildings, their fresh coat of paint doing little to hide their past as married housing for the nearby Redstone Arsenal. He parked in front of the only refurbished two-story building.

The clang of his footsteps echoed as he jogged up the metal staircase to his apartment. With a tap of the key code, he readjusted his laptop bag, then opened the orange door to greet a giant marmalade Maine Coon cat, who sat up on his haunches, waiting for him.

The rumbling of Mac's purr filled the room as Jack said, "Mac! How you doing, Buddy?" The cat rubbed against his legs, forcing Jack to sidestep the fur ball to keep from tripping as he entered. Jack let his heavy bag fall onto the worn miniature kitchen table that functioned as his desk, watching the cheap furniture wobble under its impact. Then, he tossed his coat onto the hook near the door and kicked off his shoes.

"Dude, I hope your day was better than mine," he sighed, running a hand over the tabby's soft fur as Mac answered him with a chirp. "Yeah, Guy. I could use some cheese, too."

Jack pulled a package of snack cheese from the fridge, which was almost empty, save for soda and condiments. He grabbed a can of Dr. Pepper and slammed the door shut, then used his teeth to tear open the plastic cheese package and offered Mac a small piece. The eighteen-pound cat responded with an eager bite that almost took his finger off.

"Hey! Easy, there. Did you run out of food while I was gone, or something?" He shoved the rest of the cheese in his mouth, then grabbed his soda and glanced at Mac's still-full kibble bowl. "You're making me feel bad for no reason," he said, his voice muffled by a mouthful of cheddar.

"Okay, Mac," he said, collapsing onto the worn sectional sofa that filled most of his living room. It groaned under his weight as he opened his soda with a sharp hiss. "Let's do some serious begging."

He dialed his editor's number, his anxiety increasing with each ring.

"Jack, what's up?" Isaac said. His distorted voice was a mix of his speech and the rumble of his car's engine.

"I stopped by Happily Ever After Books today, and I think I'm the wrong guy to be doing this profile. Can't you ask someone else to write it?" Jack slouched on the giant beige couch, absently rubbing the worn velour fabric. His feet rested on the scratched glass and metal coffee table as he searched for his TV remote.

"You are literally in the neighborhood, Jack. A business profile is not that hard to do. Happily Ever After Books is on-theme for Valentine's Day, and it has excellent reviews online. It will be a nice Huntsville story. Don't you need the money?"

Jack surveyed his small apartment's living area. The couch sagged, and even Mac's cat tree looked tattered and faded from years of use. "Uh…"

"What's the problem?" Isaac asked.

"The store is *pink*," Jack began, searching for reasons, "and the woman who runs it — Alison Hughes — wanders around in a frilly apron and librarian glasses with her little dust mop dog, pretending to be Snow White in a bad mood."

"What did you do to upset her?" Isaac asked.

Jack winced. "Why would it be my fault?" He retrieved a long plastic cat wand from between the sofa cushions and waved its feather toy in front of Mac.

"It's always your fault, Jack. What happened?"

Jack recounted the coffee mishap as Mac launched himself after the toy, his oversized furry body skidding across the slick coffee table, claws scraping against the glass as he slid off the end.

"It sounds to me like you can't afford to pass on this assignment."

"She's strong-arming me into writing a positive profile piece on her bookstore. I think her leverage would compromise my journalistic integrity."

With a triumphant yowl, Mac's jaws clamped down on the toy. The beast tugged while growling through a mouthful of bright feathers.

"It's a business profile about a local independent bookstore, not hard-hitting investigative journalism. Your integrity should remain intact, as long as she isn't using it as a money laundering operation. I'm home now, so I'll give you one last piece of advice: grow up and do what you have to do to keep Grumpy Snow White from garnishing your pay."

Jack ended the call with a groan, dropped to his hands and knees, and peered under the couch. Mac had knocked the remote to the floor in a fit of boredom and batted it out of reach.

"You did me dirty, Mac, as if you don't have enough toys of your own." Jack wrestled a broom from the overstuffed utility closet and swept under the couch to retrieve several dust bunnies, a plastic jingly ball, a family of well-loved stuffed mice, and a few stray socks, along with his remote. He gave the remote a quick rub on his shirt before setting it back on the end table, reminding himself to find some place safer to store it. He shoved the wand toy back into the couch cushions, leaving Mac to stare at him in wide-eyed disappointment.

"Don't give me that," Jack said, looking into Mac's sad green eyes. "You know we'll play again, later. I have human stuff to do. We have to maintain your lavish lifestyle, after all."

He finished unpacking his laptop as his phone buzzed with a new notification.

Robb: Want to watch some AL basketball tonight? I'll bring the pizza.
Jack: Sounds good to me. I have Dr. Pepper.
Robb: Soda's good. See you at 8.
Jack: K

Jack moaned at the cluttered living area, the dirty dishes piled in the kitchen sink and the food-filled pans sitting on the stove. "Plans have changed, Mac. Looks like we have some cleaning to do."

Jack

Robb Staunton arrived with the pizza just as Jack finished his frantic cleaning spree. The clatter of dishes and thuds of items shoved into the bedroom had given way to an apartment that looked — at least on the surface — tidy.

Jack buzzed him in, set plates and a roll of paper towels on the counter, and soon heard Robb's boots clang up the stairs. Mac perked up at the sound.

"Hey, Mac," Robb greeted the enormous cat, whose attention was mostly on the steaming pizza box Robb dropped on the counter.

"Hello to you, too," Jack said dryly, handing him a cold soda.

"Your human's feelings get hurt pretty easy," Robb told the cat as he opened the box. The smell of basil and hot cheese filled the room instantly.

Jack flopped onto the couch. "I've had better days. I owe a crazy book lady twenty-two hundred bucks."

"How the heck did you manage that?" Robb slid onto the couch with his plate.

Jack explained the coffee disaster. Robb listened — then burst into unrestrained laughter.

"I was hoping for help," Jack muttered. "Not a laugh track."

Robb batted away Mac's greedy paw. "What do you expect? The Love Is a Scam guy forced to work for Happily Ever After Books until Valentine's Day? This is comedy gold. Think she'll make you wear Cupid wings and a diaper?"

"I'm lucky she didn't murder me. The way she looked at me when the coffee hit that book—" Jack cringed at the memory. "She couldn't decide whether to cry or rip my head off."

"Can you blame her? That book was worth more than you are."

Jack couldn't argue on that point. "Why do I let you come over?"

"Because I buy the pizza. And because I told you back in our dorm days to go into engineering instead of journalism. Then you wouldn't be broke."

Jack chewed his crust. "Maybe Mindy would've stayed with me if I had."

Robb snorted. "Trust me, man, you were lucky she left. That woman doesn't care about anyone but herself."

"You can't think of a way out of the bookstore thing?"

"Why would you want one?" Robb leaned forward, eyes wide. "This is a gift. You write Love Is a Scam, and now you're in the belly of the beast. Buddy, you don't even have to go undercover—she's letting you in. You'll get material for months. Think about it: her entire business is selling fantasies to lonely romantics. She'll show you how she does it. You couldn't ask for a better setup."

Jack hesitated, staring at his friend as Robb flipped through the TV menu. "You really think so?"

"I know so. Be extra sorry, show up often, milk it. What's the first event?"

"Couple's book club. Some kind of Highland historical romance." Jack frowned. "What even is that?"

"Braveheart for women? I don't know. Google's free." Robb shoved Mac off his lap again. "When are you gonna teach your roommate some manners? He's too big to fight off."

"He's a cat, Robb. You don't train cats; they train you. Make them mad and they poop in your shoe. Can you imagine cleaning out Mac's poop? You'd need a forklift."

Jack shook his head, turning his attention to the TV as the game started. "Roll Tide."

CHAPTER FOUR

Extra

Sunday, January 8

Alison

The car radio played upbeat tunes as Alison drove across town, anticipation buzzing in her chest. Sunday brunch with Melissa was a ritual she refused to miss, and *Superhero Chefs* never disappointed.

The strip-mall restaurant was packed, clinking silverware and overlapping conversations rising beneath bursts of laughter. A warm smile from the host made Alison feel instantly welcome.

Melissa, of course, was already at their table—perfectly manicured hand waving in a sea of comic-themed decor. The unmistakable scent of candied bacon drifted through the air.

Her friend was effortlessly chic in a ribbed knit sweater dress, button placket neat as a runway model. Alison slid into the seat across, ordered coffee, and scanned the menu.

Despite temptations everywhere, the peanut butter cup pancakes had her name all over them.

Melissa feigned disapproval when Alison ordered. "You realize sugar contributes to aging, right?"

"I'll be lucky if I last long enough to regret it." Alison stirred two creams and a sugar into her coffee, tapping the spoon twice before setting it down.

She filled Melissa in on Tuesday's letdown with Quinn— but left out Wednesday's disaster.

Jack destroying my book is even sadder than Quinn refusing to grovel.

Melissa wrinkled her nose. "You know you're better off without him, right?"

"Of course. Let his fiancée worry about where he's sleeping. I wasn't worried about it, and look what happened." Alison rolled her eyes and nudged her glasses up.

"You had nothing to do with it."

Alison waved the thought away. "Oh, I know. I just don't understand why he bothered staying if he wanted someone else."

Melissa's glossy lips pursed. "Because he's an idiot." She shifted gears with a smile. "So, how did the Yours Truly promotion go? Did anyone guess all your beloved heroes?"

Alison's eyebrows shot up. "Two people did! I couldn't stand to choose, so I gave them both gift certificates."

Melissa smirked. "Are you in this to make a living, or aren't you?"

"I make a living," Alison argued, stacking her empty creamers. "I can share if I want."

"What's this week?"

"Couple's book club. Highland historical romance."

Melissa's eyes widened. "That's right! I almost forgot. Swords and kilts? Perfect for couples."

"I'm dressing up, because why not? I already have the outfit, thanks to Lewis and his Ren Faire obsession."

Melissa chuckled. "You kook. Too bad you can't rent a man to wear a kilt with you. That'd really draw a crowd."

Alison froze mid-sip.

Melissa's eyes narrowed as she leaned in toward Alison. "You're hiding a man from me?"

The waitress set their food down before Alison could answer. Melissa's filet mignon gleamed atop crispy home fries and scrambled eggs. Alison's plate was a wobbling tower of pancakes layered with chocolate whip, crumbled peanut butter cups, and glossy sauce, flanked by potatoes and candied bacon.

Alison smiled. *This is at least two more meals. I love when someone else does the cooking.*

"No, not in the romantic sense," she said finally, sawing into the pancakes. "It's Jack Morrison. You know: Love is a Scam?" She explained the entire disaster to her friend.

Melissa nearly dropped her fork. "You're making *that* Jack Morrison work for you? How do you know he won't sabotage the events?"

"Because he doesn't want me to drag him to small claims court. I don't expect much in person, but at least he can handle the event listings. And a positive profile in *Alabama Online* won't hurt."

Melissa closed her eyes in bliss at the first bite of her filet. Then she opened them. "What's he like in person? A bitter old man?"

Alison laughed. "No, he's a bitter man our age who doesn't fold his laundry. Dresses like college never ended, except he swapped jeans for chinos, probably at HR's insistence. I doubt he owns a comb. At least Bella likes him, so odds are he's not a serial killer."

A forkful of pancakes made Alison shimmy in her chair with delight.

"He sounds like a man-child. And you're considering putting him in a kilt?"

"He should thank me. Kilts make any man look good. He'll hate it, which suits me fine. After ruining my book and accusing me of using AI to write my letters? He deserves every ounce of suffering I can serve."

Melissa grinned. "Which is the bigger crime—the book or the accusation?"

"The book, no contest. But the AI insult wasn't excusable either." Alison speared a potato, making a mental note: *rent Highlander kilt ensemble after brunch.*

"You should stretch the theme all weekend," Melissa suggested.

Alison nodded. "Why didn't I think of that?"

"Because I'm inspirational," Melissa said, flicking her hair with a playful smile. "Send me your list. Let the Queen of Extra show you how it's done."

Alison

Stuffed from brunch, Alison texted Jack from her car in the
grocery store parking lot:

> **Alison:** What are your measurements?
> **Jack:** What?!
> **Alison:** For clothes. Waist, shirt, shoe size.
> **Jack:** Why?
> **Alison:** Because you owe me $2200.
> **Jack:** Fine. Waist 30. Inseam 32. Large shirt.
> Size 10 shoe.
> **Alison:** You don't know your shirt
> measurements?
> **Jack:** Why should I? I wear large shirts.
> **Alison:** Is that what you wore on
> Wednesday?
> **Jack:** Probably.
> **Alison:** Thanks. See you Friday night.

Her phone rang.

"Don't think you can talk your way out of this, Jack,"
she said by way of greeting.

"Yeah, I know. Look, I've been thinking. I feel terrible about ruining your book, and I want to do my best to make it up to you. If you want, I'll help the entire time your bookstore's open until Valentine's Day. Whatever you want."

Suspicion prickled Alison's neck. "You're not planning to sabotage me, are you?"

"No! I don't need more debt hanging over me. If I spend extra time at the store, I'll understand your business better. My profile will be stronger, and it'll help me repay you."

What's his angle?

"Alison? Are you there?"

"I could use the help," she admitted, "but if you screw me over, Jack Morrison, so help me—"

"I won't. It's hard enough making an honest living doing what you love. I wouldn't take that away from anyone."

"You mean that?"

"Of course."

Alison exhaled. "Fine. Meet me in the Lowe Mill parking lot Wednesday at ten. Have you sent the event blurbs yet?"

"Not yet. Planning to tonight."

"Good. Change them. This week is Highland Romance Week. Twenty percent off Scottish romances, online and in-store. Special Blind Date With a Book packages. Got it?"

"Got it. Is that why you wanted my measurements?" His tone turned wary.

"You're catching on," Alison said, "but at least you won't be stuck in a frilly apron. See you Wednesday."

Melissa was right: being extra just took practice.

She dropped a quarter into the grocery cart slot and added shortbread cookies in case she couldn't track down a local baker. Back home, Bella inspected every bag while Alison unpacked.

"You're so nosy!" she said, clipping Bella's leash for a twilight walk. The little dog spun in circles at the word *out*, making Alison grin despite the cold.

That night, she placed the order for Jack's kilt rental: a Morrison tartan ensemble, medium shirt. Hopefully, it would fit better than the sloppy, faded T-shirt he'd worn the day they met. After grooming Bella, Alison unearthed the pup's plaid bows and collar from the accessory drawer.

Her own Highland dress waited too. Lewis, her Ren Faire-obsessed ex, had convinced her to buy the costume— only for her to realize she hated watching turkey-leg-eating strangers ogle fairy girls in polyester wings. She'd recycled the outfit for two Halloweens since.

At least this weekend, I'll finally make good use of it. And this time, it's for my promotion, not someone else's obsession.

CHAPTER FIVE

Men in Kilts

Wednesday, January 11

Jack

Alison didn't notice Jack parking his truck beside her hatchback on Wednesday morning. Earbuds in, she stared at her phone while Bella panted beside her. Jack rapped on the driver's window.

Alison jolted when Bella exploded into a frenzy of barks by her ear. She yanked out her earbuds, exhaled hard, and opened the door.

"Sorry," Jack said. "Didn't know how else to get your attention."

"Don't blame yourself. I should've taken the earbuds out."

Bella didn't wait for permission. She clambered over Alison with an "oof" from her stomach and launched at Jack. Alison rolled her eyes. "Honestly. No couth. That's why I lock your butt up during store hours."

Jack caught Bella's leash and scratched her head as she wagged herself nearly airborne. He smirked. "Quite the outfit for this event."

Alison climbed out of the car and straightened her long brown skirt and white puff-sleeved blouse, then shoved her glasses up her nose. A black corset and plaid sash defined her waist.

On anyone else, that would actually be…hot.

She popped the hatch to reveal stacked boxes and a garment bag. "Let's haul these to the shop." With practiced ease, she unfolded a red nylon-and-steel cart. "My little red wagon saves the day again."

When does she have time for all this?

"Is this an everyday thing? An every *week* thing?" Jack kept Bella's leash while she loaded the wagon.

"Not exactly. My promotions are more elaborate the first six weeks of the year, but the wagon hauls out my online orders daily. It's worth its weight in gold."

Alison pulled the garment bag free, opting to carry it instead of balancing it on top.

Jack eyed it warily. "Is that my costume?"

She cleared her throat before raising her chin. "I'm in costume. You're in proper attire. I even ordered a tartan for your family name. You'd be welcome at any Highland Games. Treat it nice—it's a tux rental, not a Halloween costume."

Jack grunted, tugging the wagon up the ramp to the elevator. "You take this seriously, don't you?"

"We're catering to historical fiction fans. They'll know if something's wrong, especially a Highland kit."

On the second floor, Alison handed him the garment bag as she fumbled with her keys. "I've pulled a bunch of books for the displays. Once you've changed, you can help set up. Bathrooms are down the hall, and I sent you a link on how to wear the kilt."

Jack grimaced with dread at the garment bag. "People are going to stare."

"That's the point. And it won't be because you look silly. Women love men in kilts. Entire calendars are devoted to it."

"Are you objectifying me?"

Alison flashed a sweet smile. "Bless your heart, Jack. I could never objectify you. Now go change; we've got work to do."

She slipped inside, shutting the door behind her. Jack stood alone in the hallway, garment bag dangling, wondering how the hell he'd ended up here.

Jack

Twenty minutes later, Jack left the bathroom clad in a kilt and tunic. The garment bag and his street clothes were tucked under his arm.

"You made me wear rental shoes," he muttered when he stepped back into the shop. "Like I'm bowling."

Bella bounded toward him, a whirlwind of fur and licks, as if seeing him for the first time.

Alison glanced up from tugging at a tartan tablecloth. "You like bowling?"

"That's irrelevant. I'm wearing rented shoes." He gestured sourly at his feet.

Her gaze swept over him. "You look good. Sporran's at the right height. Stash your clothes in the office—back by the aprons—and help me finish these tables."

"I look ridiculous." Bella's trot matched his heavy strides. "I offered to go beyond what you asked, and you made me look silly."

"You said you'd do anything I wanted," she called as he tossed his clothes into the corner.

Why did I say that?

"The guy in the video wore a dress shirt," Jack grumbled as he stomped out. "Why am I in a blouse?"

Alison spun, hands on hips, eyes narrowed over her glasses. "One, it's not a blouse, it's a Highland tunic. Big, burly men throw logs around in that outfit. Two, you're supposed to look like you're on the moors, not headed to a cocktail party. And three, you didn't give me jacket measurements anyway, even if I'd wanted to order a dress kit, which I didn't."

Her stance radiated challenge.

Jack blinked, then shrugged. "You really do put a lot of thought into this."

"Of course I do. Now stop complaining about wearing the nicest thing you've probably had on in years and help me set up before we open."

With a weary sigh, she returned to draping plaid cloths while Jack stacked books featuring shirtless men in kilts.

These books are so tacky. How does she convince men to read them with their wives and girlfriends?

Alison's phone alarm chimed. She tucked Bella behind the baby gate, unlocked the door, and pulled her sandwich board into the hall. Jack glanced around at plaid-draped tables. Bagpipes played softly, and Alison glowed with energy.

"It's fantastic," she said, beaming.

Jack had to admit, the Scottish vibe worked. "You sell much online earlier this week?"

"Lots. My newsletter and socials do most of the winter lifting."

"Why don't people just order from the big guys?"

"Because I offer what they don't: clubs, surprise packages, a little fun in the mail. And some folks like sticking it to The Man."

"How can you run a romance bookstore if you hate men so much?"

"I said The Man, not men. When I dislike people, it's on an individual basis, unlike someone who writes a weekly column tearing down love."

"My column's not about hating love. It's about the industry around it."

"Like romance bookstores?" she shot back.

"Maybe."

"I run an honest business. What's wrong with wanting to make people happy?"

"Your books give readers unrealistic expectations."

"What do you read?"

"Science fiction."

"Does that give you unrealistic expectations about photon blasters and rocket ships?" Alison slid a basket of local shortbread onto the counter, arranging them neatly with a bakery sign.

"Of course not, but sci-fi doesn't always promise a happy ending, either."

"You think my customers don't know happy endings are fantasy? Most of us have enough experience to know better. And those who don't will learn soon enough."

Ouch.

The bell jingled. An older woman breezed in, coffee in hand.

"Welcome to Happily Ever After!" Alison called brightly.

The woman's gaze raked over Jack. A glint of mischief sparked in her eyes. "Highland Romance Week? What fun. And you—look at you, so handsome. Is that your kilt?"

Jack shifted. "Nah. She rented it."

"Too bad. It suits you." She turned to Alison. "All Highland romances are on sale?"

"Yep. Everything in a kilt—except Jack. He's not for sale."

She winked at Alison. "I wouldn't let him go either."

Alison cleared her throat, heat rising in her cheeks. "He's seasonal help."

The woman nodded, scooped up three books and two cookies, and checked out, still grinning at Jack before leaving.

Jack rounded on Alison. "'He's not for sale'? Do you hear yourself?"

"She looked ready to peek under your kilt. I diffused the situation before I had to throw her out for harassment. You aren't for sale, are you?"

Her deadpan stare made heat crawl up his neck.

"You would've kicked her out?" he pressed.

"Of course. Nobody harasses my employees," she said evenly. "Except Bella. Now pet her before she explodes."

Jack

Jack spent the rest of the day monitoring the front of the store while Alison meticulously folded books into colorful wrappings, adding stickers, bookmarks, and handwritten thank-you notes before setting them in tissue-lined boxes for shipping.

"Wednesdays are slower," she explained, "but that gives me time to fulfill online orders."

"People pay extra for this?" Jack asked, watching her fuss with ribbons.

"It's like receiving a gift, even when you buy it for yourself. Because the details are a surprise, it feels personal. Don't you like when someone puts extra effort in for you?"

"But it's not a gift," he countered. "They're paying for it."

"My effort adds value. Would you rather unwrap a present or rip open a plastic bubble envelope with a dented book inside?"

Jack shrugged.

"You don't believe intention counts? My customers love knowing someone went to trouble for them. It makes them feel special."

"They're not special to you," Jack muttered, bending to scratch Bella's ears. "You've never even met them." One look at Alison's scowl made him regret the words.

Alison's tone sharpened. "They *are* special. My customers trust me not to pawn off AI garbage. They choose me over billionaires, which keeps this place alive. I appreciate every one of them—and this is how I show it. If you don't get that, it's not meant for you."

By evening, fatigue crept into her movements, though her voice remained bright when the bell above the door jingled.

"Welcome to Happily Ever After!" she called as Robb walked in, eyebrows raised at Jack's kilt.

"I wanted to see what my boy was up to," Robb said, shaking Alison's hand. "Robb Staunton. Friend of Jack's."

"Alison Hughes. Jack's been a huge help—and an even bigger distraction for Bella." She nodded toward the dog, who was whining for more attention.

Robb grinned, crouching by the gate. "Jack! Don't let Mac near this one. He'd eat her as a snack."

Alison's brows shot up. "You have a dog?"

"An eighteen-pound cat," Jack corrected.

"A *house* cat?"

"Maine Coon," Robb supplied. "A monster. Friendly, but a monster. Long fur, giant paws, big ears, fluffy tail."

Alison tilted her head, appraising Jack anew. "A cat guy. That makes sense."

Jack crossed his arms. "What's that supposed to mean?"

"You're good with animals, but you don't know much about dogs. Cat guy fits. Better than one of those men who claim anything under forty pounds isn't a real dog."

"Is she a real dog, though?" Robb teased, petting Bella. "She looks like a wind-up toy."

"You should see her on a walk. But then she finds something revolting to eat and — trust me — illusion shattered. Real dog."

Robb straightened, grinning. "I need a picture of you in this kilt."

Jack frowned and narrowed his eyes. "Why? So you can roast me for years?"

"No, because you haven't looked this put together in over a year. Even your shirt fits."

"It's a medium," Alison chimed in.

"I told you I wear a large," Jack snapped.

"That's why I rented a medium. So it *would* fit."

Robb shook with stifled laughter as he lifted his phone.

"Take the damn pictures," Jack muttered. "I don't want you hanging around all weekend."

Click. Robb snapped a few shots — Jack scowling, then grinning despite himself. He added one of Alison beside Jack, tidying her sash, then another of Alison alone, Bella perched in her arms beside the display.

When Robb left, Alison told Jack he could change back. "I'll wash the shirt and socks. Just because you look like you're out on the moors doesn't mean you should smell like it."

"Uh, thanks." Jack averted his eyes as he handed her the outfit.

"Coming back tomorrow, or have you had enough of being extra sorry?"

He squared his shoulders. "I said I'd come."

"I was just reminding you—you don't have to go beyond our deal. You're welcome to learn as much as you like about bookselling, but if it gets in the way of your livelihood, you're free to walk."

"I'll let you know," he said, his voice softer now.

Alison flicked off the fairy lights as Jack hauled her wagon into the elevator and down the creaky ramp. Bella's paws clicked alongside them as they crossed the pitted lot.

Alison folded the heavy cart into her car, then smiled. "Thanks, Jack. You were a great help today. See you tomorrow?"

"See you tomorrow," he echoed, watching her load Bella before sliding behind his own wheel.

Jack

Jack entered his apartment to find Mac planted on the kitchen table beside his laptop, green eyes locked on the door.

"Get off there. Are you nuts?" Jack scolded, already knowing the cat wouldn't move.

Mac meowed loudly, tail flicking. Jack sighed, shed his coat and shoes, then scooped up the oversized feline. Mac poured from his arms onto the floor like a sack of fur, then purred and followed him to the cabinets.

The microwave beeped as the water boiled for noodles. Jack realized the cat's real problem when he found the kibble bowl empty.

"Sorry, buddy." He filled it, watching Mac inhale food like he hadn't eaten in a week. "Not so fast—you know what happens."

Jack settled onto the sagging sofa, springs groaning beneath him, noodle cup steaming on the end table. He dialed Robb.

"Still wearing that kilt?" Robb answered without a hello.

"I wouldn't be caught dead in it outside the store. You're deleting those pictures, right?"

"Nope. Already shared them."

"Online?!"

"In the group chat. Haven't you been getting the messages?"

"My notifications have been off. I don't want to see this, do I?" He rubbed the back of his neck.

"The guys think you and Alison make a cute couple. You should read it."

Jack groaned, his head tipping back to the ceiling. "The crazy book lady and me? Why would you do that?"

"Because you *are* a cute couple, with your matching outfits and everything."

Jack shoved Mac away from the noodles. "You were right: that store is the belly of the beast. Everything has to be cute—her pink store, frilly aprons, gift-wrapped mail orders with stickers and thank-you notes, her fluffy dog with tartan bows. I bet she lives in a little pink house with a white picket fence."

"If she does, she's a catch. Have you seen property values?"

"Back off, Mac, that's boiling," Jack warned as the cat sniffed at the steam.

"And her dog likes you," Robb said. "That puts you halfway there."

"Alison hates me. She made me wear a kilt."

"Do yourself a favor: Google men in kilts."

Jack flipped his phone to speaker and searched. "Did you know there's a local window-cleaning company called that?"

"Photos, Jack."

He tapped the tab and grimaced. "Ugh. I've seen enough shirtless guys on book covers today. Alison even had to shoo an old woman away from checking under my kilt."

"Material for your column already: female gaze as sales gimmick. And it's only day one."

Jack smirked despite himself. "I called to make sure you didn't share those pics anywhere else. I'm hanging up before Mac steals my noodles. He's already bolted his dinner, and—"

Too late. From the bedroom came the unmistakable sound of feline gagging.

"Mac, no!" Jack sprinted in, vaulting a laundry heap, but not fast enough. The cat coughed up dinner all over Jack's stocking feet as he was lifting him off the bed.

"Why?" Jack groaned, peeling his socks off while Mac purred, unconcerned. After mopping the mess with a paper towel and pulling on clean socks, he returned to find Mac's head buried in the noodle cup.

"That was my last one!" Jack yanked it away. "Thanks to you, I've lost my appetite anyway. You're the worst roommate ever."

Mac looked up, chirped sweetly, and licked his whiskers.

Jack sighed and scratched Mac's chin. "If I can't have these noodles, nobody can. You'd probably eat them anyway and keel over. Don't you care about your health?"

CHAPTER SIX

Insta-Love

Friday, January 13

Alison

For the third morning in a row, Alison waited for Jack in the chilly Lowe Mill parking lot.

Even if this is the only weekend he shows up every day, it's more than I expected.

She kept her earbuds out, scrolling through promotion stats while Bella left nose prints on the passenger window. Highland Romance Week was already a smash hit. Additional sales had covered Jack's kilt rental before she'd processed Monday's orders.

Melissa is a genius.

The familiar rumble of Jack's pickup made Bella whine and scratch at the door, her whole body vibrating. Alison tucked away her phone and adjusted the pleats of her great kilt before Jack could witness her wrestling the fabric.

Bella practically howled when Jack parked beside her.

"Will you *try* to control yourself?" Alison muttered as she caught the leash before Bella bolted. "You just met him. He's not even a dog person."

"Ready for our second busiest day?" she asked as Jack opened her hatch.

"Sure." He tugged at the wagon to remove it from the car, but he had to readjust his grip before it budged.

Alison bit back a smile as she handed Jack the leash and easily lifted the wagon from the car.

Note to self: don't ask him to help move a body.

Jack grunted. "I had it."

"I know. Just didn't want you scratching my paint."

"It's heavy." He eyed her. "How do you make it look easy?"

"I own a bookstore. Lifting heavy things is part of the job."

She clicked the cart open and dropped her purse, laptop, and the tote with his laundered shirt and socks inside.

"Why are we hauling this now if it's empty?" Jack asked, half-amused, half-annoyed.

"So I have it ready tonight. I'm not dragging the cart up two flights for fun."

"Oh. Right." He glanced at the bright winter sky. "Nice day. Supposed to hit forty."

"Except it's Friday the 13th."

"You don't strike me as the superstitious type."

"I'm not, but other people are. Just wait: customers will act weird. It's like the full moon, but self-inflicted."

"The full moon thing's a myth," Jack said as he pushed the elevator button.

"Maybe, but every time I get swamped by irrational people, I find out it's a full moon. Correlation may not equal causation, but sometimes it's a reliable predictor."

His brow arched as the elevator doors closed.

"What?" Alison shot back. "You think because I read romance I can't read anything else?"

"What did you study?"

"Business Administration. Community college. Low debt—that's why I still have a store."

"Smart," he said as they stepped out.

Alison blinked at the unexpected compliment.

Bella matched Jack's stride like she'd been his dog forever, toenails clicking on the worn wood floor. "I'm still paying my student loans off. Couple more years left."

"Ugh. Nobody warns eighteen-year-olds they're signing up for thirty years of payments," she said as she unlocked the shop.

Jack closed the door and let Bella loose. The dog sprinted around the perimeter, tags jingling.

"She's fast," he said.

"Remarkably so for such short legs." Alison stowed the wagon, then handed him the garment bag with kilt and accessories, along with the tote of laundered clothes. He took them without a single eye roll.

As Jack disappeared to change, Alison scowled at Bella in the warm morning sunlight. "He's not your human, you know. Don't get attached. Insta-love is not a good look."

Alison

A young blond woman entered the store pushing an enormous stroller. Inside, a toddler slept, lips parted, head lolling.

"Welcome to Happily Ever After. How may I help you?" Alison asked.

"Where's your children's section?" The woman's sleek ponytail bobbed as she scanned the shelves.

"Sorry, no children's section. This is a romance bookstore."

"So you hate children?" Her glare snapped to Alison like a spark ready to ignite.

Unfazed, Alison smiled. "Not at all. I just find most children aren't interested in romance."

"How am I supposed to shop if you have nothing to keep Hunter occupied?"

Alison gestured to the stroller. "Looks like Hunter's already occupied. Can I help you find something?"

"No. I don't shop where children aren't welcome. Expect to see it on Yelp." She spun the stroller toward the door, wheels rattling on the way.

"Have a nice day," Alison called. The boy never stirred.

Behind her, Jack muttered, "What was *that*?"

Alison shrugged and rolled her eyes as she returned to the office to wrap another stack of books.

A few customers later, an older woman bustled in, her lacquered hair helmet unmoving as her suspicious eyes locked on Jack's legs.

"Is this one of *those* stores?" she asked.

"Welcome to Happily Ever After's Highland Romance Week!" Alison said brightly. "How may I help you?"

"Are you about to start drag queen story hour?"

"We don't have a story hour, ma'am. This is a romance bookstore. Can I help you find something?"

"I won't buy from a store that employs cross-dressers." Her sneer flicked toward Jack's kilt. "Men shouldn't pretend to be women."

Jack went rigid, eyes darting between Alison and the customer.

Alison's voice snapped, sharp as glass. "Then why are you wearing pants?"

The woman blinked. "Excuse me?"

"Why are you wearing pants if you're against cross-dressing?" Alison repeated, her tone cutting.

"These are women's pants," the woman sniffed.

"And that's a man's kilt. Either way, what he wears is none of your business. You're welcome to leave now, and never come back."

"You're asking me to leave?"

"No, ma'am. I'm *ordering* you to leave. You wouldn't buy from a man in a skirt, and I won't sell to a hateful bigot. So we're agreed. Thank you."

Jack's mouth fell open as Alison marched the woman toward the door. When it shut, she shook her head. "Too bad we don't have mall cops. I'd pay money to see one drag her out, hairdo and all."

"You kicked her out," Jack said, still pale.

"I'm sorry I couldn't *shove* her. Hard." Alison slammed a pile of books onto a shelf. "Told you today would be weird."

Later, a middle-aged man walked in, his eyes snagging on Jack's kilt with a quick intake of breath.

"Welcome to Happily Ever After," Alison said before Jack could get a word out. "It's Highland Romance Week. Interested in the displays?"

"You're Scottish?" the man asked with a grin, tilting his head toward Jack. "I've never seen you at the Highland Games."

Jack shrugged, clearly uncertain what to say.

Alison stepped in smoothly. "His family is, some generations back. This is a promotion outfit. This is Jack."

"Mike," he said, shaking Jack's hand with a smile before turning back. "My wife sent me for some Highland books."

"Then you're in luck." Alison gestured toward the display tables. "Everything is pulled out for you. Easy shopping."

Mike left with four books and two shortbread cookies.

When the door shut behind him, Alison caught Jack's unsettled expression. "Relax," she said dryly. "Mike's married. He wasn't asking you out. Besides, his wife Eva reads smut so filthy you'd need a microscope to find the plot. Those books were for him."

Jack gave an awkward grunt in response, which made Alison smile despite herself. "You might actually enjoy the Highland Games, though. They're in May."

Another customer arrived, a woman with a straight brown bob and windblown bangs. Adjusting her glasses with a motion eerily like Alison's own, she declared, "I'm looking for a book. It's blue. Dark blue."

Alison squeezed past Bella's gate. "Blue, huh? Paranormal romance?"

The woman nodded. "Yeah."

"Werewolves, vampires, or demons?" Alison looked at the ceiling in thought.

Narrowing her eyes, the customer eventually answered, "Demons."

Alison snapped her gaze back to the woman's face. "Red hair on the cover? Black?"

She looked unsure. "Maybe purple?"

"Ah—this one." Alison plucked a fat paperback off the shelf and handed it over.

The woman gasped. "Yes! Thank you."

"First in a series. Take a picture for next time." Alison shot a smug glance toward Jack, almost a bow.

"Good idea." She glanced at the counter. "Are those shortbread cookies?"

"They are, and very good ones, at that."

"Two, please."

"I'll add the bakery's card. Thanks for stopping in." Alison rang her up, then leaned against the counter as the doorbell chimed behind the customer.

"Jack, check when the next full moon is, please."

He fished his phone out of the sporran. His eyes were wide when they met hers again. "Tonight."

"Figures." Alison sighed. "Friday the thirteenth and a full moon. No wonder."

Alison

With book club half an hour away, Alison asked Jack to move the bulky display tables toward the walls. As he condensed the displays to half their number, Alison rattled a cart of folding chairs down the hall. The metal chairs clattered against each other with each thump of the wheels over the floor's imperfections.

Jack cocked an eyebrow as she brought the large, heavy cart to a stop outside the store. "Why didn't you ask me to get it for you?"

"I would have had to explain where it was," she said, catching her breath. "It was just as easy for me to fetch it. We only need eight chairs."

And you might not have been able to handle it on your own.

Jack grunted with effort as he hefted pairs of heavy steel folding chairs. Alison unfolded them with a sharp *snap* and arranged them in a tight circle.

"I'll return the cart," she said. "Be right back."

When she returned, a lovely red-haired woman was posing with Jack, who was holding Bella like she had known him all her little doggy life. Her friend took their photo. "One more," the photographer said as the redhead's attention drifted toward Alison.

"Oh, can you join us? I hope you don't mind that I borrowed your husband," she said, waving Alison over. "I love a man in a kilt."

"If you've borrowed Jack," Alison said with a wide grin on her face as she stepped into the frame for a few pictures, "it's because he let you. We're not a couple. All I ask is that he returns the kilt on time."

"I didn't know you could rent kilts."

"I guess you can rent about anything," Alison remarked, watching the women shower Bella with affection as Jack held her. Bella, always ready to meet new people, perked her ears, gave a happy sniff and then licked the air between them.

"Anyway," the redhead asked Jack. "Do you have any recommendations from your Highland romance books?"

He held Bella like a football, his other hand raised in surrender. "You'll have to ask Alison. I'm just learning about the place."

The women exchanged goodbyes with Bella before leaving half an hour later with bags full of books, bookmarks, and stickers.

Alison smirked at Jack. "Did she slip you her number?"

"What? No, I'm not here to pick up women," Jack said, tucking his chin as he gave her an irritated scowl.

"I know you're not, but I thought she might have given it to you, anyway. I mean, you're obviously not with someone right now," Alison said, tidying the remaining displays.

"How would you know?"

"Because I read your column. If you were in a happy relationship, you wouldn't write such things."

Jack huffed. "And if I was in an unhappy relationship?"

"Are you in an unhappy relationship, Jack?"

"No, I'm not."

"See?" When Melissa arrived, Alison hugged her on sight. "Jack! I want you to meet my favorite non-relative on the planet. This is Melissa."

Jack appeared frozen as Melissa, in a long red wool dress coat, took off her black leather gloves and tossed her long blond hair over her shoulder. With her hand outstretched, she said, "So, this is the famous Jack Morrison. Pleased to meet you."

"Uh, hi," he replied with a nervous tremor in his voice as he took her hand.

"I see she got you to wear the kilt. It suits you. How do you like the attention?" Her dazzling smile, the same one she gave everyone, seemed to leave Jack breathless.

"Thanks," he mumbled, "I'm fine. How are you?"

Unable to contain her laughter, Alison turned away. Melissa had stopped another man dead in his tracks.

"I'm doing well. Are you helping with the book club tonight?"

"I, uh, haven't had a chance to read the book," he said, his face flushing crimson.

"Well, the book is pretty chonky. You can borrow my copy if you want, after tonight."

"You're in the couple's book club?" Jack asked, his shoulders slumping with visible disappointment.

"I'm the honorary single. Alison allowed me to participate this month after she told me which book it was.

I read it ages ago, but I was obsessed. How has the promotion been going?" Melissa asked.

"Swimmingly, right, Jack?" Alison said, waiting for Jack to pull his tongue off the floor.

"Yeah. Swimmingly," he said.

"Great. Do you need any help, Alison?" Melissa inspected the circle of chairs now taking up much of the space. "I wish there was a better way of doing this."

"If I used another room, people wouldn't shop," Alison said, biting her lower lip in thought.

Melissa shook her head. "That's no good, then. What if we did two rows facing each other?"

Alison planted her hands on her hips. "I don't know. Wouldn't it feel like a face-off?"

Mischief filled Melissa's eyes. "Ha! We could make women sit on one side, and men on the other, facing their partners."

Alison chuckled. "I say we stick with a circle. It's already set up."

Melissa studied the chairs, her brow furrowed in concentration, then a slow expression of satisfaction spread across her face as she nodded, the way she always did when she arrived at the best possible solution. "Square it. One couple per side. Do you have tea back there?"

"Of course. Make some for yourself, but don't tell anyone where you got it. The folks down the hallway would have my head." Alison clapped her hands once before she repositioned the chairs.

Melissa, if I could borrow your head for about an hour a day, nothing would stop me.

"They use the same tea bags you do, and they charge three dollars for it. They have no right to complain."

Melissa squeezed past Bella into the office, shedding her coat, to reveal a pair of gray wool slacks and a crisp white shirt. "Anybody else want some?" While waiting for the kettle to boil, she ruffled Bella's floppy ears.

"No, thanks. This outfit is sweltering. Do you want some tea, Jack?" Alison asked, trying to snap him out of his stupor.

He's as bad as Bella.

Alison welcomed the three couples as they arrived for the book club, joining them once everyone was present and settled. After the meeting concluded, Melissa stayed behind to help Alison and Jack restore order to the bookstore. As they finished, Alison sent Jack to change into his street clothes. She watched him turn the corner to the bathroom, then turned to Melissa.

"You gonna give him your number?"

"Why? Do you hate me, now?" Melissa asked.

"He's following you around like Bella. He's smitten," Alison said. "I want to see how the *Love is a Scam* column would change if he was dating you."

"That adoration would last about two weeks before he started complaining about how long I take to get ready and how I spend my money, because he has none of his own. I know his type. He likes fancy women who are also low maintenance."

Alison wrinkled her brow. "There's no such thing."

"Exactly. I'd rather be alone." She extinguished the fairy lights and bagpipe music, then helped to load the wagon. The snap of Bella's leash seemed loud in the now-silent store as they prepared to leave. Jack, breathless and flushed, rushed back to meet them, placing the garment bag into the already-cluttered wagon.

As they rode the noisy old elevator to the parking lot together, Melissa picked up Bella to pet her.

"So, uh, do you visit the bookstore often?" Jack asked Melissa as she scratched behind Bella's ears.

"I'm around," Melissa said, keeping her attention on the dog.

"Oh. Well, I'll see you around, then?" he said, his tone reminiscent of a teenager. Jack's sweatshirt, jacket, and worn chinos hung on his frame. Melissa's polished look made her seem otherworldly in comparison. Alison felt a twinge of pity for the man, despite herself.

"Sure," Melissa said with an indulgent smile. Once they reached the parking lot, Melissa embraced Alison, then gave Jack her copy of the book and a little wave before heading to her car. Alison caught him peeking inside the front cover to see whether Melissa had written her contact information there. She hadn't.

Jack's eyes followed Melissa's car as she drove away, seeming to hold him captive. With a curious tilt of his head, he asked, "How do you two know each other?"

"We went to high school together," Alison said. "We were inseparable. Yes, she was always that gorgeous."

"Was I that obvious?"

"You have to ask?" She touched his upper arm and looked directly into his eyes. "I'm going to say something that might sound unkind, but Melissa would tell you the same thing, herself: she is high maintenance. Not that she's looking for someone to take care of her. She pays her own way, but she wouldn't make herself more convenient for anyone."

"Pot, meet kettle," Jack replied.

"I am not high maintenance," Alison said. "I am also not inflexible."

"Right. Sure." Jack helped her load the car before saying goodbye to the dog.

"See you tomorrow?" She closed the hatch.

"Yeah, tomorrow," he said, watching her open the car door for Bella.

CHAPTER SEVEN
Until You Say Yes

Saturday, January 14

Alison

Alison's key grated in the shop's lock Saturday morning as Jack lifted the garment bag from the wagon.

"One last day in the kilt," she said. "Do you think you'll make it?"

"Piece of cake," he declared, his voice echoing in the long hallway as he headed to the bathroom.

Bella tugged at her leash, her whole body straining as she tried to follow him, her ears perked and tail wagging.

"He'll be back, you little traitor." Alison dragged the dog into the store, Bella's nails scraping against the floor as she struggled against Alison's pull.

Thanks to Melissa, the displays were in order, and everything was ready to open. Alison set up her laptop on the worn desk in her office, ready to process online orders.

Jack dropped his clothes in a clump in the office corner when he returned.

"What's up for today?" he asked, affectionately smooshing Bella's face the same way Alison did.

"Saturday is the big day for foot traffic."

She packaged the remaining online orders amid the growing murmur of customers.

Jack was the big draw. Alison was certain he'd been photographed more in the past week than he had the entire previous year, posing with women and couples who almost always left carrying at least one new book. Alison sold out of her shortbread cookies from the local bakery after lunchtime, replacing them with free grocery store cookies on a plate.

Later in the afternoon, Quinn walked through the door, his shirt and slacks perfect and his tie knotted, the faint scent of his cologne lingering in the air. The man was much too dressed up for a Saturday afternoon.

He must be going out tonight.

"Ali," he said, his voice smooth as he gave Alison a warm smile.

"Hi, Quinn." The sound of a name attracted Jack's attention. Alison didn't need an audience for what she knew would happen next, so she invited Quinn into her office, telling Jack to call if he needed her. Bella, a furry blur of excitement, bounced against Quinn's legs, yipping as they squeezed past the baby gate. The store's bustling sounds were muffled by the bookshelves walling them off.

You have terrible taste in men, Bella. Too bad you don't shed. His pants could use it.

Alison invited Quinn to sit, and he pulled a stool up to the worktable, eating up the space with a classic man-spread. Her eyelid twitched as she fought the aching need to roll her eyes.

"Cute costume. Who's your friend out there?" He rested his forearms on the table as a slow grin spread across his face.

"That's Jack. He's helping out until Valentine's Day."

Who knows what kind of havoc Quinn would wreak if he discovered the author of the Love Is a Scam column was standing in my store?

"That's so sweet of him. Are you two…"

"Not that it's any of your business, Quinn, but we're not. He's a seasonal employee. Can you please get to the point?"

Quinn pouted, his lower lip protruding as he tucked his chin to give Alison sad eyes. "Is that any way to act, Ali? I'm trying to be cordial, here."

Alison released a sigh, knowing that Quinn couldn't be rushed. He had to play out his entire scenario, complete with dramatic pauses. She let him continue like an ad she couldn't skip. His eyes darted around the crowded office, doubtless searching for the turquoise leather book, but Alison had stashed it where she couldn't see it every time she entered the area. The man would have to turn the office upside-down and shake it to find the volume.

"You can't have my book, Quinn, and you're taking up my time on a Saturday afternoon. I have things to do." Alison tried to push her glasses up her nose, but she found they were already sitting in the right spot.

"It's not your book, though, and I would like it back."

"That's too bad, isn't it? If you talk to a lawyer about it, you'll discover that it isn't yours, and it probably never was. I imagine you talked your mother into letting you give it to me, and I don't see her demanding it back." She took a long sip from her giant tumbler, wishing with all her might that Jack had spilled his coffee on Quinn's expensive outfit instead of her beloved copy of *Pride and Prejudice*.

Quinn ran his hands through his perfect hair, let out a heavy sigh that seemed to fill the room, and then stood to leave. She ushered him through the gate, the metallic clang cutting through the bustle of the store. He turned at the door with a determined glint in his eyes and said, "You know, I'll keep coming back until you say yes."

Alison wished she had followed him to the door. She had denied herself the satisfaction of slamming it on that arrogant jerk. Instead, she turned to Jack, who had seen too much, and gave him a look as cold and dark as the bottom of a well.

If it hadn't been for Jack, I wouldn't be going through this right now.

He busied himself with a feather duster she had left behind the counter.

Jack

Jack watched Alison stare after the man as he left her sight, her shoulders tense.

Quinn. Quinn who?

She had dragged the man to the back office to avoid anyone witnessing their conversation. Both when he arrived and when he left, he had sounded so casual, so sure of himself.

You know, I'll keep coming back and asking until you say yes.

The remark had made Alison furious, and Jack didn't know why. One thing was certain: she didn't like that Jack had heard a word of it.

Alison stormed to her office without a word. Even Bella begged for distance, whining at the gate, but Jack didn't dare approach to free her. After ten minutes of tension, Alison exited the office, exuding the kind of calm that covered a landmine.

"Jack, would you mind taking Bella out for a quick walk, please? I'd do it, but I want to be here if I'm needed."

"Sure. Yeah," he said, taking the dog's leash. Once Jack left sight of the store, he inhaled all the air in the hallway. "Come on, Bella," he said as he led the little dog down the stairwell. "I needed a break, too. I didn't know your mama could be so scary. Who's Quinn, and how can he still smile after that?"

Bella kept her secrets, doing her business for Jack outside and attracting plenty of attention with her plaid bow, her long, flowing tail, and her kilt-clad human in tow. Jack was unsure whether steering additional customers to the store was the best idea at that moment, but he decided the alternative would be far worse.

When they returned, Alison was back to herself, assisting customers until half an hour before closing. She re-shelved the Highland romances in their normal places, folded the tartan tablecloths, and shared the remainder of the grocery store shortbread cookies with Jack before setting the plate aside to take home.

By the time 7 pm arrived, Alison had retrieved the kilt ensemble from Jack, readied the store for closing, and even packed the wagon. The lights were out, and so were they. "Do you have everything? I'm ready for my weekend," she said to Jack, handing Bella's leash to him as she locked the door.

"Yeah, I'm ready," he said, amazed at the speed with which she was able to close the place.

"Thank you for your help this week," Alison said as they entered the elevator. "You are welcome to come extra days next week, but you don't have to."

So, I was a help?

"You told me that," he said. "I told you I'll be there. What is next week, anyway?"

"We have a literary speed dating event Friday night," she said.

"How is that different than regular speed dating?"

"It's for people who like books," she said as they walked to the parking lot, clouds drifting across the night sky. "Maybe you could participate."

He sidestepped the suggestion. "Why don't you?" He let Bella lead him to Alison's car.

"I'm running it." Alison raised her voice to be heard over the wagon as it rattled along the rough surface of the parking lot.

After they loaded the car, he opened the back door for Bella to hop in and said goodbye to the dog as Alison buckled herself in. "Bye, Jack. I'll send the online calendar information to you tomorrow."

"Okay," he said as he climbed into his truck. She waited to drive away until it started.

Jack

Jack called Robb after pulling out of the drive-thru. He could no longer wait to describe Alison's run-in with Quinn.

"It was bizarre, the way she acted when that rich-looking guy walked in, like she was hiding something. And then how she was furious when he said he would keep coming back until she said yes."

"Maybe she has personal business that she didn't want to share with a journalist she barely knows," Robb said, his voice hollow through the truck's hands-free system. "That's the problem with you people. You don't know how to mind your own business."

"You people?" Jack asked, the accusation clear in his voice.

Robb chuckled. "I thought that would get you. Still, you're not being a journalist. You're being a busybody."

"It's my job. That's not a normal thing for a man to say." He pulled some hot, salty fries from the bag and shoved them into his mouth at the stoplight.

"Why don't you ask her about it?" Robb asked.

"Because the look she gave me practically reduced me to cinders. I was afraid to ask anything."

"Pft. And you were the one who fantasized about doing foreign correspondence in war zones when we were in school. It's not like she's armed, probably. She gave you that look because you were eavesdropping. Don't tell me you're going to start peeking through her windows."

"Of course not, but if I'm going to write a business profile, I want to make sure I'm writing it about a legitimate business. What if it has to do with money laundering? How else can you make a living running a romance bookstore? Maybe she's tucking something extra into those book packages. She's hiding something."

"You're the one with something to hide. Wouldn't it be easier to ask her out?" Robb asked.

"What? Ask her out to get information? That would be unethical."

"Dude, you're an idiot. This Quinn guy probably wants to buy her store, and she's either sick to death of him, or she's trying to run up the price. Let it go. You're writing a lifestyle column for *Alabama Online*, not doing investigative journalism for the *Washington Post*. If you want to know more about her business, keep working there. If you want to know more about *her*, ask her out on a date."

Jack pulled up to the gate outside his apartment complex, trying to dig his card out of his wallet. "You don't get it. I don't want to date her. There's something going on, and I want to figure it out. I saw the kind of business she runs. This dude has no interest in buying her out. No rich guy wants to work that hard just to eke out a living." He shoved the card into the passkey slot, and the gate rolled open.

"You're ridiculous, and you're home. I heard the gate. Take some time to sort yourself out, Jack. Go tell your cat I said hi."

"Fine." Jack shoved some more French fries into his mouth. Parking in front of his apartment building, he grabbed his burger bag and ran up the staircase, the metal clanging beneath his feet.

"Mac," he said, opening the door to see the cat on his haunches waiting for him. "I'm here. Let's have some dinner, and we'll watch the rest of the game together."

Flicking the end of his long, fluffy tail, Mac chirped and dropped onto all fours.

Jack tossed his jacket over the back of the kitchen chair and kicked off his worn gym shoes with a thud. He held his precious burger and fries out of Mac's reach, then grabbed a can of soda from the refrigerator. The couch springs threatened to give way when he dropped into his seat. "Hang in there," he muttered to the sofa, resting his elbow on the bare spot in the arm's velveteen as he ate fries from the bag. "You can't retire yet."

He gently shoved Mac's face away from his dinner. "Cats don't even like fries, you goof. Eat your own food."

As he dug the remote out from between the sofa cushions with his non-greasy hand and turned on the game, even basketball and Mac parading in front of the television couldn't stop the replay of Quinn's words that kept running through his head.

You know, I'll keep coming back until you say yes.

CHAPTER EIGHT
Rabbit Holes

Wednesday, January 18

Jack

When Jack met Alison in the parking lot the following Wednesday, it seemed almost odd to see her in regular street clothes, wearing a wool coat over a sweater and slacks instead of her Highland outfit. She picked her way around the potholes filled with water from the previous night's rain, carrying Bella in her arms. Handing the dog to Jack, she opened the hatch, the hinges creaking a little as she pulled out her wagon. With a snap, she opened it, dropping her laptop bag inside with a careless gesture.

"Bella's already had a walk this morning, and she's less than thrilled with the wet parking lot. If you don't mind, you can save me the trouble of cleaning her feet again by popping her into the wagon," Alison said, nodding toward the dog cradled in Jack's arms, trying to lick his face.

Bella snuggled into his arms, making no move to hop down to the bumpy wagon. "I think she won't mind if I carry her."

"I warned you about her," Alison said. "She'll wrap you around her little paw."

"I noticed." He walked alongside Alison and her red wagon to the elevator. "Did you have a good few days off?"

"I didn't have any more time off than you did, but yes, Sunday off was nice, and sales have been good. Melissa was a genius, coming up with the novella and anthology promotion to go with the literary speed dating event this weekend. Thanks for sending out the notices. I may have to cancel Friday's speed dating event if I don't have more men sign up."

"That's too bad," he mumbled.

Why would men sign up for an event at a romance bookstore, anyway?

"What's your column about this week?" she asked.

"Er, diamonds," he said, setting Bella down when she began growing restless.

"Diamonds? Too easy," she said with a dismissive wave as they boarded the elevator.

His head swiveled toward Alison, a flicker of surprise in his gaze. "You think so?"

"I'm surprised you hadn't covered it before, honestly. They're not rare, and you can make perfect ones in a lab. There are prettier substitutes, and anyone telling you to spend two months' salary on anything is taking you for a ride."

"You basically quoted my entire article," he said as they walked the empty hallway from the elevator to the shop door.

"I hope not. You didn't forget the part about them funding wars, right?" Her keys jangled against the door. "And the cartels? And South Africa?"

"You know a lot about it."

"It's a rabbit hole, and I like rabbit holes. I also hate bullies. There are some businesses that cater to bullies, and that's one of them. Just because I'm a romantic doesn't mean I support everything sold to me in the name of love." She took off for the back office at a quick clip, her damp rubber-soled leather shoes squeaking on the floor as she went.

Jack released Bella, and the jingle of her collar announced her customary lap around the store before she bounded back to him, tail wagging.

"Ready to set up displays? I have all the novellas and anthologies pulled and placed next to the tables." Alison looked every bit the Southern lady in her dainty sweater and string of pearls. She almost seemed overdressed for the artsy Lowe Mill setting.

"Did you sell many of your 'buy four, get one free' packs?" he asked.

"Several," she said. "Most people don't think hard enough to figure out that it comes to the same twenty percent off I had on my Highland romances, but romance readers are notorious for being voracious, reading them all like they're eating popcorn. My great grandmother used to go through two or three grocery store novelettes a week. It's much less expensive for me to sell five books to one person than it is to sell one book to five people, so we're all happier for it."

"Novelette? I thought these were novellas," he said, arranging the slim volumes.

"Correct." She began reciting as if Jack had flipped a switch. "Novelettes are between 7,000 and 17,500 words. Novellas are between 17,500 and 40,000 words. Novels go from 40,000 to 120,000, and epics come in between 120,000 and 200,000. Tomes have to literally stun an ox in field testing."

Jack looked up to see her smiling at the display she was working on.

She's a book nerd's book nerd.

"You have that memorized?" he asked.

"That's the set of numbers I have memorized. There's no law, but those are generally accepted lengths." Her mouth quirked when she looked at him. "Have you ever considered writing a book, Jack?"

"I'm a journalist. Of course, I have," he mumbled, returning to the display.

"Have you started?"

"I did, once. Life got in the way." His voice was quiet.

"Don't feel too bad. That's what happens to most novels. Life gets in the way, and they never make it past the first few chapters. First drafts end up stuck in laptop folders, gathering digital dust. Ninety-seven percent of all novels never make it to the end of their first draft. I can guarantee that there is no source for that statistic, but it's the one you'll read everywhere."

He'd never heard Alison string that many sentences together at once. "Sounds like you're speaking from experience."

"Of course, I am. Those who can, do. Those who can't, sell. What kind of book is it?"

"Was. Nothing important, just a science fiction book."

"Did you just say science fiction isn't important? Jack Morrison, take that back, this minute. You've just called Jules Verne, Ursula K. Le Guin, George Orwell, Margaret Atwood, and Kurt Vonnegut unimportant."

He chuckled. "I'm sorry, I didn't mean it that way. It's just that I'm not them."

"And you never will be, if you don't finish your book. You have to finish it for people to trash it. Talk to any of these authors." She gestured around the shop.

"That's not true. Mine was trashed well before it was finished." He finished his last display as Alison's phone alarm signaled the start of the day, and Jack opened the shop door, dragging the heavy sandwich board into the hallway.

"You let your mother read your book before it was finished? You should know better." She powered up the register after dropping Bella behind the gate with a plop.

"It wasn't my mother; it was my girlfriend," he said. "My *ex*-girlfriend."

"Thank goodness for the 'ex' part, if she trashed it before your first draft was even finished. Your first draft is supposed to be terrible." Alison said. "Was she a sci-fi fan?"

"No, but I trusted her opinion."

"But now she's your ex, so maybe you should try again. How far did you get?"

Jack shrugged. "About halfway."

"Halfway is good. You should get life out of your way so you can at least finish your first draft. Nothing like writing those last two words…I hear."

"What about you?" he asked. "Were you writing a romance?"

"Yeah. Life got in the way." From across the register, she offered him a genuine smile of camaraderie.

"Is he your ex too, now?" Jack asked.

"Yes. I trusted him, too." She wrinkled her nose as if the memory conjured an odor other than the pleasant new-book smell that filled the store.

"When are you starting up again?" Jack asked, a challenge in his voice.

"Good question. I'll share my first half if you share yours," she said.

A shot of fear hit Jack's stomach. He had expected Alison to squirm at the suggestion. "I don't know."

"Come on, Jack. I'm a very low-risk reader. I'm familiar with science fiction, and you have nothing to lose by letting me read it. Hey, you don't even like me."

"That's not true," Jack argued.

"Really? With my silly pink bookstore full of romance books and my frilly aprons? If you like me, it's for my silly, fluffy little dog."

Jack felt a stab of regret at what he had said to Alison before he had known her, despite her reminding him in jest.

It's true that women forgive, but don't forget.

"You have a leg up on me, at least," she continued. "You've taken writing classes at a fancy state school. All I've taken are business composition courses at the local community college. I dare you."

"You can't get me with that," he sputtered. "I'm not a kid."

She gave him a playground smile, all narrowed eyes and tight, curled lips. "I double-dog dare you."

"I'm filing a complaint with the labor board." He grabbed the feather duster from behind the checkout counter and began dusting the bookshelves to change the subject. "My boss just said that if I show her mine, she'll show me hers."

Alison gasped, scandalized drama spilling from behind her uncharacteristically southern demeanor. Her accent grew country-thick. "How *dare* you? And standing in the middle of the Sweet Romance section, at that!" She clutched the pearls at her neck.

"I have to hand it to you. I've never seen anyone actually do that before," Jack said, tearing his gaze from her parted lips as the first customer of the day entered.

Jack

That night after work, Jack's microwaved frozen dinner filled the apartment with the flat aroma of processed food. Sitting before his laptop at the kitchen table, he had to shoo Mac away three times before the cat gave up. Two limp, razor-thin mushroom slices lay atop the bland gray meat sporting artificial grill marks, a reminder of what the photo on the box promised. The mushy, bright orange mac and cheese that accompanied it left a salty aftertaste in his mouth. He repeatedly purchased the unappetizing meal, enticed by the image on the bright orange box and driven by habit and impulse.

Why would I bother to disappoint a girlfriend? I disappoint myself, even when I go grocery shopping.

Focused on his upcoming column about online flower ordering, Jack mindlessly ate as he reviewed customer complaints about skimpy arrangements of drooping roses and watched video clips on services he hadn't used himself.

Why am I doing this? Florists are a scam. I don't have to go into online ordering to find the bad actors in this one.

Still, some people liked flowers. Even if Jack didn't, it didn't mean people shouldn't get what they paid for.

Jack was about to leave his fork in the sink after dinner when he remembered the ant problem. With a sigh, he tossed it into the dishwasher, recoiling from the fetid smell of long-dirty dishes that hit him like a wall. He scoured the apartment for additional glasses and dishes and started the dishwasher before he forgot again.

So that's what that smell was.

Unable to hear the video over the clamorous dishwasher chugging through its cycle less than five feet from where he sat, Jack instead checked his email. Despite his turning down her challenge to swap manuscripts, Alison had sent her unfinished first draft to him.

An icy dread wormed through Jack's brain. Although he was curious, he knew that opening the attachment would obligate him to share his precious manuscript with Alison. What would his reaction be if her writing was unreadable? Even worse, what if her book was so incredible that it became an award-winning best-seller? He would be the guy who spilled coffee on her favorite book *and* wrote a bad, unfinished novel. He shook his head and closed her email. It was too risky.

The phone rang, cutting through the clatter of the dishwasher and his thoughts, and he retreated to the bedroom to answer Robb's call.

"Hey, Robb. What's up?"

"Just wanted to know what your first working day in pants was like. Wait, are you in the shower?"

"It's the dishwasher."

"You should go into the bedroom so you don't have to listen to it."

Jack sighed. "That's where I am. The day went okay. Nobody asked to take my picture with the dog."

"I told you to buy that kilt. What did you argue about today?"

Jack set the phone down and began folding the basket of clean laundry that was blocking his way to the bed before Mac could fill it with orange cat fur. "Nothing, but she wants to see my book."

"You finished it and didn't tell me?" Robb's outburst was so intense that Jack winced at the blast through his earbuds.

Jack groaned, wanting to avoid another discussion about the incomplete manuscript. "No, I didn't. It's still where it was when Mindy read it. Alison and I both admitted we had unfinished manuscripts, and she offered to trade. I tried to put her off, but now her manuscript is in my inbox."

"Is it any good?" Robb asked.

Jack pulled all the pants out of the laundry basket. He'd waited too long to fold the laundry, leaving it a wrinkled mess. "I'm afraid if I read it, I'll have to send her mine."

"So what? If she likes it, she'll respect you more and you'll feel better about it. If she doesn't, there's no problem, since you don't like her, anyway," Robb said.

Did I say that? He flapped the pants open, making them as smooth as possible.

"I'll think about it." Even Jack knew he sounded unconvincing. "Anyway, her promotion this week is literary speed dating. She has short fiction on sale and an event set to go on Friday. She'll probably cancel the Friday event because not enough men have signed up."

"Literary speed dating? That sounds hilarious. How many more men does she need?" Robb asked.

"I didn't ask," Jack said. "It's not like I'm signing up. I don't want a girlfriend, and I'm working the event, if it happens."

"You should put a call out on the group chat. It would be something different to do on Friday before we go watch the game, and it would liven up what might otherwise be a boring day for you."

"Maybe. She would be pretty disappointed if she had to cancel the event. Alison puts a lot of work into her promotions." He hung up the pants, hoping the rest of the wrinkles would fall out.

"Do it! I'll even sign up," Robb said.

Apprehension tickled the back of Jack's brain. He couldn't put his finger on why, so he dismissed it.

"Okay. I'll do it," Jack said, sending the event description and link to the chat.

"And you should read her manuscript. If it's awful, you don't even have to tell her you read it. She'll never know, and you'll get a look inside her head."

"Do I *want* that?"

"It would be more revealing than an interview," Robb replied, "but that's just me. You can keep dusting bookshelves, wondering what's going on upstairs if you want, instead of taking the easy way out."

"You're right, she doesn't have to know," Jack said. "I need to do some actual work. I'm researching online floral ordering services."

"Sounds riveting. Have you ever thought about broadening the scope of your column?"

"I haven't run out of material so far. Talk to you later."

After folding the rest of his clothes, Jack returned to his computer. Ignoring the clattering dishwasher, he reread Alison's email. At the end, her attachment taunted him.

"Fine," he said, downloading the file.

Jack

Jack didn't like romance books.

His attempts to find good urban fantasy novels were thwarted by dark monster romances. Every book contained excessive steamy sex scenes. When he skimmed over the bedroom scenes, the books' narratives became disjointed and incomplete, like reading abridged short stories.

Porn for women. Not that there's anything wrong with that...

The dog-eared Highland romance Melissa lent him lay on his nightstand, unopened, despite the rave reviews the book club men gave it for its political intrigue and immersive historical setting.

Still, reading the first chapter of Alison's manuscript wouldn't hurt. It would give him an idea of her writing style and ability. She was an avid enough reader that she might have some latent talent, even if, by her own admission, nobody had taught her how to plot a book.

Jack took a deep breath and opened the document, steeling himself for a painfully twee, purple prose-ridden reading experience.

After finishing the first chapter, it nearly killed him to admit that Alison had a good hook. An unemployed art restorer returns to her hometown to sort through her late father's estate. In his desk, she discovers two journals. One is her father's, and the other is an antiquated journal that hints at a valuable artifact her father was secretly searching for, and may have found.

One more chapter wouldn't hurt.

A former FBI agent turned private investigator appears, claiming her late father hired him to locate the artifact. The heroine remains unconvinced. Tensions flare as she finds herself both drawn to him and unable to fully trust him.

Okay, so that was three more chapters. At this point, I may as well finish.

When her home — her late father's house — is ransacked, the perpetrators leave a threatening message warning her away from searching for the artifact. It's clear someone dangerous is also searching for it. As the two work together to trace her father's last steps, they uncover a deadly black-market network willing to kill for the relic. She is at the top of their hit list.

And then it stopped.

"That's it?" Jack slammed his laptop closed with a groan. "Why did Alison *stop*, Mac?" The manuscript had all the hallmarks of a first draft: typos, scene inconsistencies, weird transitions, and superfluous text, but its raw brilliance shone through.

He couldn't send his manuscript to her.

Jack paced his small apartment. Her character development was impressive; her dialogue was plot-driven and realistic. Her prose was lyrical, and the plot was unique and full of suspense.

How could this be a romance? At this rate, she'll be on a book tour while I sit at my wobbly kitchen table writing about fraudulent lingerie subscription services.

He hadn't checked the time in hours, but a quick look revealed that it was nearly midnight. The dishwasher had finished hours before, and he hadn't written a word of his column.

As he tossed and turned in bed that night, Jack tried to imagine the man who had criticized Alison's manuscript so harshly that she gave up on it. He must have been jealous of her talent. Jack was jealous of her talent, but he wouldn't be jealous enough to sabotage work like that.

Lulled by Mac's rumbling purr as the cat kneaded his paws on the pillow Jack used as a claw barrier, he drifted off to sleep. Mac's soft warmth was, as always, a comforting presence.

CHAPTER NINE

Be Nice or Leave

Friday, January 20

Jack

On Thursday, Alison hinted but didn't directly ask Jack about her manuscript. He may have been stalling her, but he wouldn't lie about it when she eventually lost her patience and asked.

Mindy had been correct. Jack's manuscript was dog water, and Alison would insist that he send it to her after he admitted to reading hers. If he gave himself a few more days, he might adjust to the idea.

Friday morning, she went over the plan for the speed dating event, which involved six-minute conversations between potential couples in rotation, so everyone would talk to each potential match. Finally, participants would submit a list of the people they wanted to see again. If the feeling was mutual, Alison would share contact details.

Jack's friends had said it sounded like an entertaining warm-up before watching basketball at the Scoreboard that night. All the singles in the group signed up for it, promising to make Jack's evening a success.

"I couldn't believe all the last minute male registrants! Did you send this to a different online events list?"

"Er, no," Jack said, hoping she wouldn't ask whether he recognized anybody on the list. He pictured them taunting him from the tables.

"I was lucky they let me set up in the hallway," Alison said. "There's not enough room in the store."

She rolled the heavy folding chair cart to the front of the store, her feet skidding as she pulled the clattering cart to a stop. Then she requested Jack's help to retrieve three folding tables, which they set up in one long row.

While Alison smoothed the white polyester tablecloths over the hollow plastic tables, Jack set up the metal chairs. Their sharp clangs echoed through the long, wide hallway as he arranged three sets at each table.

His gaze followed the row of tables. "How would six minutes be enough to determine whether you were interested in someone?" he asked, following Alison as she placed a small globe with a battery-powered candle at each station.

She raised an eyebrow at him. "You're telling me that, after six minutes of pointed conversation with a person, you wouldn't be able to decide whether you wanted to learn more about her? It took all of five seconds for you to fall all over yourself for Melissa."

Jack felt his face grow hot. "That was just…"

Alison smirked. "It was just enough time for you to decide you liked her." Alison tipped her head to the side as she regarded the row of tables, then rushed to her office, returning with some "reserved" table tents. "We don't need cafe customers spilling coffee on our speed dating tables."

"I said I'm sorry," Jack snapped.

Alison's brow furrowed in confusion before she realized what she had said. "I wasn't referring to you, Jack. I didn't want people messing up my tables, is all."

He cleared his throat. "Oh. I guess I'll go in and straighten the store."

"Monique!" Alison said. "I'm so glad you could help tonight."

Jack turned to see a woman with dark skin and short, gray-kissed coiled hair in her late forties approaching from the stairwell. She wore brown slacks and an olive-green stretchy blouse underneath her black, hip-length jacket. Stopping to assess the speed dating setup, she pursed her full, plum-coated lips and pulled them to the side in thought.

"What? What's wrong?" Alison asked, pushing her glasses up.

Monique shook her head, her lips pressed together. "Nothing is wrong," she said after a moment. "You just need some more signage, is all. I'll go make it."

"Thanks. Monique, this is Jack Morrison. Jack, meet Monique Willis. If I could afford an assistant manager, she would be it."

Monique narrowed her eyes to assess the man for a moment. "Jack. You're the *Love Is a Scam* guy who—"

"Yes. Now I'm in bookstore purgatory, trying to make up for it."

"I'll get rid of this coat and make up those signs, then." Monique rushed past Jack, her gold earrings glinting in the light. "Pleased to meet you," she called over her shoulder.

"Likewise," Jack called after her, unsure whether she heard him, or even cared, by the time the word left his mouth.

Jack

Everything was in perfect condition when the speed daters began arriving at 5:30. Alison greeted everyone at the front of the store, Jack registered them in the center, and Monique managed customer service. Monique seemed to know the store's stock as well as Alison did, and most of the customers she spoke with made a purchase or two.

At one point, he turned his head back from watching Monique pitch a book to see Melissa standing before him at registration, her blonde hair cascading about her shoulders, with her red wool coat flaring around her.

"Hi, Jack," she said. "You're going to get me all fixed up, right?"

"Yeah, sure," he answered, blinking in the sunshine of her smile and feeling terribly underdressed in his wrinkled chinos and polo shirt.

"Great! I miss the kilt, by the way," she joked as he handed her a nametag attached to a bag containing the event instructions, a notepad, a golf pencil left over from the "Yours Truly" event, a bookmark, and a 20% off coupon for the store.

"You, too," he said, realizing only after she had walked away that his reply made no sense.

Why didn't I sign up when Alison asked me to?

As Melissa disappeared into the group of people, Robb approached, still dressed for work in a shirt and tie.

"Jack! It looks like Alison put you to work on this one. Will you have to help put all this stuff away, too?" Robb grinned through his neatly trimmed beard as Jack handed over his bag and checked his name off the list.

"Probably. It's one of the few stipulations of this deal that I'm required to fulfill. I don't blame her for roping me into it. There's a lot more physical labor involved in these events than I imagined. If there's one thing women know we're good for, it's carrying stuff. Are the other guys coming?"

"As far as I know, they are." Robb leaned in toward Jack. "Did you read it?"

Jack scanned the room until he spotted Alison near the door and cringed. "Yeah. We can talk about it later."

Robb grimaced. "That bad, huh?"

Jack shook his head, the motion barely perceptible. "I can't talk about it right now."

"You didn't tell her you read it? Ouch," Robb said as a hand clapped onto his shoulder from behind.

"Robb, I thought we were here to meet women, not talk to the help," Gary said. Jack gave the tall man with sandy blond hair a reproving look when Monique looked in their direction.

"You said your name was *Gary*?" Jack said, checking the list for his name until Monique looked away. "Don't get me in trouble," he hissed when the coast was clear. "I know Alison and Melissa are sharp, and Monique seems to be on the same level. If the three of them think I tried to sabotage an event, they'd tie me up, cover me in honey, and toss me on a fire ant mound."

"You're exaggerating," Gary argued.

"Am not," he murmured through gritted teeth. "You saw Alison. She's that little woman in the pink shirt and the glasses. If I don't behave, she'll sue me to get the money I owe her. The blond standing next to her is her best friend. She's a pharmacist, and smarter than the three of us put together. The woman could poison me, and they'd never figure it out. That older lady over there in the green? I just met her tonight, but she's been watching me like I'm about to steal the pretty pink paint off the walls."

"Where do I pick up my nametag? I want to meet that tall blond in the black," Brian said as he pushed his way in, raising his bushy eyebrows and stroking the stubble on his chin as Kareem stood behind, pretending not to know him.

"Brian, was it?" Jack said in a voice loud enough for Monique to hear as he checked his friend's name off the list, then handed his bag to him. "You should go *mingle*," he said pointedly, dismissing the three men as Kareem allowed a pair of women to approach the registration table before him.

By six, when the event was supposed to start, Jack had checked in seven women and eight men, four of whom were his friends. He expressed his concern about the no-shows to Alison, who gave him half a shrug and told him she expected a few not to show up.

As he watched his friends mingle, Jack's reservations grew. Robb and Kareem were behaving themselves, but Gary and Brian were bordering on participating in what locals called "horsejackery," despite some sharp looks from Jack. Even worse, Monique seemed to catch on to the fact that Jack's friends had overrun the event, if her glances toward him were to be taken seriously.

Jack had not yet learned what Monique's day job was, but her glares reminded him of the ones he received from his mother when she realized Jack and his brother Paul were up to something. He could tell Monique was not a woman to be underestimated, and he had the feeling she would rat him out to Alison in a second. That was the last thing he needed.

Brian was being particularly bothersome toward Melissa, who had already had her fill of his forwardness. Jack was about to ask Robb to drag Brian away when Alison called the event to order.

"Welcome, y'all, to the first literary speed dating event sponsored by Happily Ever After Books," she announced, her Alabama accent a touch more pronounced than usual. "I see many of you have brought your favorite book with you so you'll have something to talk about. I know you've read the rules on the website, but we'll go over them again, just in case you've forgotten. The women will sit on one side, and the men will switch seats with each date when I call time. Please note the first name and participant number of the persons you would like to know better. If they have also expressed an interest in you, we will send you their email information. Remember, following strangers to the parking lot without their permission is called *stalking*. I will call the cops and sic my dog on anyone who does that, hear me?"

The group laughed, but Jack could tell that Bella was the only thing Alison was joking about. That woman would fight a stalker on her own rather than risk the little dog in her office. The police would have to rescue creeps from *her*. He smiled at the image.

"Alright, now," she continued. "Places, everybody. Remember, be nice, or leave!"

Alison

Alison noticed Jack keeping tabs on the four men who were obviously his friends. Robb and Kareem were charming, but Brian and Gary were treating the event like a joke, their loud, obnoxious behavior making those around them cringe.

Jack nervously twitched in the background, occasionally approaching the men before recoiling. His hesitant steps betrayed his desire to avoid a confrontation. He also watched Monique, who picked up on Jack's easy camaraderie with half the men. Monique had often told her that men sensed and feared women who had raised sons. Alison stifled a chuckle at Jack, who looked terrified that Monique might pull him away by his ear.

Alison called the end of the first date, watching the men switch places. Brian and Gary, seated beside each other, began horsing around again, interrupting each other's conversations and pretending to fight over seats. With a sigh, she decided to let it go. The men were showing who they were, and neither one was harassing the women. Monique, however, gave Jack a withering look, implying he was to blame for their actions.

After Alison called the end of the second date, Brian and Gary's childish behavior escalated, and their noise became disruptive. Two minutes into the third date, Jack abandoned his hesitation. He grasped the two men's shoulders from behind, squeezing until his fingers turned white. With a tight jaw and a reddened face, Jack murmured something into their ears.

The exchange took less than twenty seconds, but the two men sat straight in their chairs, reminding Alison of children who had just been pinched for misbehaving in church. She disguised her amusement with a hostess smile, turning her attention farther down the set of tables as Jack, averting his eyes, hurried into the bookstore to avoid further scrutiny.

Meanwhile, Robb shared a lively conversation with Melissa. His gestures were animated as Melissa leaned on her forearms, beaming as she responded. Alison almost hated to call an end to the third date.

The rest of the hour passed without a hitch. Even Brian and Gary seemed to enjoy their mini-dates once they behaved like adults. After the last date, Alison held up her phone.

"This concludes the First Annual Literary Speed Dating Event from Happily Ever After Books! Congratulations, Speed Daters!" The group greeted her announcement with polite applause. "We still have a little time left before closing. Please make sure your name and email are at the top of your sheets before you hand them to Jack at the check-in table, and we'll go through them all to notify you of your matches. Feel free to do a little shopping if you wish before we close at seven. Monique, the lady in green, will be happy to help you."

Alison

Melissa laid a hand on Alison's arm to get her attention among the group's noise as participants filled the store. "Is the chair cart still in the same place?"

"You needn't do that," Alison replied, shaking her head. "Jack and Monique are here."

"It's no trouble." Melissa held out her hand, palm up. "Keys?"

Alison dangled the keychain by the proper key and handed it to her friend, who strode toward the storage area in two-inch heels, leaving several disappointed suitors in her wake.

Always leave them wanting more.

Melissa returned with the cart a few minutes later, digging in her heels to stop it without skidding. All four of Jack's friends were already folding the chairs. She loaded the chairs onto the cart, easily keeping up with the four men as Jack tucked candle globes into a cardboard box.

He shooed Alison into the store to assist her remaining customers. By the time the store closed at seven, Melissa and the five men had finished cleaning up.

Alison took the keys from her friend, who waved goodbye before disappearing down the stairs. Alison then thanked everyone and took Bella's leash from Monique after locking the door.

"Wait a minute," Gary said. "I want to meet Bella. I've heard so much about her." Alison raised an eyebrow at Jack, who answered her with a little shrug. Gary kneeled down to let Bella lunge toward him, her entire rear end swaying with joy. "Sorry I was such a goober," Gary said, looking up at Alison and Monique. "I don't know what got into me."

"Me, too," Brian added. "When Jack got mad, I realized I was being a jerk. We can act like adults, I promise. I hope we didn't do too much damage."

"You're fine." Alison resisted rolling her eyes. "I appreciate you coming. We couldn't have held the event without you." She turned to Jack. "I assume you five are going out somewhere? You should get moving before the game starts."

"You sure?" Jack asked.

"What did you think we did before you showed up?" Monique asked Jack with the first smile she had ever offered him. "Go watch your Alabama basketball game, wherever it is that lets you hooligans hang out."

"Okay, see you tomorrow?" Jack asked Alison.

"If you want. Monique will be here tomorrow, so you should take the day off to write your column, or something. Last week's was good. What is it this week?"

"Online floral ordering."

"Too easy, again. How will I hate read you if I keep agreeing?" She chuckled. "Enjoy the game."

The men headed down the staircase, ribbing Robb about Melissa, as Alison and Monique pulled the wagon full of orders to the elevator. Bella tugged at the leash to follow her new friends.

"I thought for sure that man had tried to undermine your event," Monique muttered as the elevator doors closed behind them.

Alison shook her head. "It wouldn't have happened, if not for him inviting his friends, even the *goobers*." She quirked her mouth at Gary's word.

"I had my doubts until he set those two straight," Monique replied as they waited for the elevator to open. "He seems decent enough, even if his mother never taught him to fold his laundry."

Alison checked the parking lot to make sure all the men were gone before she answered. "I think he's depressed. Anyone who writes a column called Love Is a Scam and has an ex who stopped him from finishing his book has a right to be."

"You ought to know. Your ex stopped you from finishing your manuscript, and I'm still salty about it." Monique followed Alison to her car. "I want to know how it ends! Do you even know?"

"I know how it ends. I may start it up again, but once you stop, it's hard to restart." Alison loaded her car. "I couldn't have done tonight without you. Have a good night at work, and I'll see you tomorrow."

"My pleasure. Now, go relax. You work too hard this time of year."

Alison let Bella into the back seat, then buckled herself in and drove home. She left almost everything in the car before walking the dog for the last time that evening.

"Bella, baby, do you think he isn't interested enough in my little romance manuscript to read it? Or do you think he read it and thought it was so awful that he's pretending he hasn't? I shouldn't have sent it to him." She pushed her glasses up as the desire to take it back made her stomach twist, as it did every time it rose to mind.

As Bella's toenails tapped on the sidewalk and the chilly night wind found its way into her ears, Alison recalled Jack's dismay at his friends' misbehavior.

He not only invited his friends to help my event, but he confronted them in public to save it. That wasn't just thoughtful; it was downright sweet. Who knew that Jack Morrison had the capacity to be sweet?

Jack

Robb leaned toward Jack to be heard over the lively crowd as the five friends watched the game at the Scoreboard. "How bad was her manuscript, that you didn't even tell her you read it?"

Jack finished a Buffalo wing before answering, dipping it into creamy blue cheese dressing to tone down the heat, then wiping his fingers before taking a sip of his sweet tea. He kept his eyes on the oversized television screen in the dark sports bar as he talked. "Her manuscript wasn't bad; it was great. The plot wasn't even a romance, like she told me it was. It's a suspense with a romantic subplot. She has no business writing a suspense that good, what with her sweater sets and pearls and her little fluffy dog."

"It was great, and you didn't tell her you even read it? Are you trying to kill her, or something?" Robb shook his head.

Jack turned to him, defensiveness tightening his shoulders as he shifted his feet on his high-top seat's rung. "What do you mean? I didn't tell her I hated it."

"No, instead you made her feel like you couldn't be bothered to open it."

The bar erupted in cheers as Alabama scored again.

Jack grimaced, recognizing the sinking sensation in his stomach. "If I admit I read it, then she'll push to read my manuscript. Mine is hot garbage next to hers. Mindy was right; I'm nothing but a hack."

"Mindy isn't just a hack; she's a petty, malicious hack. She tore you down out of jealousy."

Jack picked up another wing, dipping the sloppy piece of chicken into the blue cheese dressing, hoping the game would distract Robb before he spoke again.

"Gogogogogogo!" Kareem shouted from two seats away.

"You know I'm right," Robb said, underlining his previous statement.

"Mindy doesn't have anything to be jealous of anymore, does she?" Jack's bitterness welled inside him as he pondered his half-eaten wing.

"That doesn't make her less of a hack. Don't you think it would be better to get an opinion from someone better than Mindy? Besides, it's only fair that you send your draft to Alison in return."

Jack's head snapped toward Robb. "Did you encourage me to read that so you could guilt me into sending my manuscript to Alison, you *tool*? Why would you do that?" Jack wiped his hands on his last napkin and waved the server to the table to ask for extras.

"Because you really did want to read it, and I want you to finish your book. That novel is too good to be abandoned, and you're too good to give up." Robb's eyes grew wide as Kentucky's large forward charged toward the basket, scoring as if Alabama's center wasn't even there. "NO!"

"What if *she* hates it, too?" Jack asked, scowling at Robb, who was too preoccupied with the game to notice.

"She won't. Alison likes you," Robb said, shoving a French fry in his mouth.

"She does not. That woman would rather take the $2200 I owe her from my hide. Why would you say that?"

"Didn't you notice how she smiled at you when you were putting Gary and Brian in their place? If there hadn't been a crowd, *that woman* would have hugged you. Besides, you were cute in your matching outfits last week."

Alabama's center blocked Kentucky's small forward when he dodged toward the basket, prompting a round of shouts from the bar.

"I didn't see anything. How would you know? You couldn't see me talk to those knuckleheads." Jack ignored the reproving look Brian gave him from his other side.

"Melissa did color commentary when you read Gary and Brian the riot act, and I watched Alison's face the whole time. Besides, if she hated you, she wouldn't send you her manuscript."

"She doesn't like me, but even if she did, that doesn't mean she would like my work," Jack said, picking up his last wing and using it to scoop the remaining dressing from the serving cup.

"Suit yourself, but you should at least tell her you liked her book," Robb said. "It would be the honest thing to do."

He had to pull out the honesty card, the jerk.

"Ugh. You're right, it would be the *honest* thing to do." Jack wanted to pour his tea over Robb's head.

"By the way," Robb said, eating another fry as he stared at the screen, "it would be great if you went in tomorrow. I'm dying to know whether Melissa chose me. And don't you have any clothes that don't look like you've slept in them? You're supposed to fold them when you take them out of the dryer."

CHAPTER TEN

Burrs Under the Saddle

Saturday, January 21

Alison

It was still dark the next morning when Alison opened her laptop and read an unexpected email from Jack that made her heart race.

> Alison-
> I'm sorry I didn't tell you sooner, but I really enjoyed your manuscript. In fact, it's amazing. You should finish it so I can read the rest.
> The reason I didn't say so before is because now I owe you mine, so here it is.
> —Jack

Amazing? He can't mean that. Jack's a professional writer.

It was only 6:30, hours before Alison had to leave for the store. The aroma of freshly brewed coffee filled the living room as she settled onto the couch with her laptop, ready to dive into Jack's manuscript.

His novel was set two hundred years in the future. People buy and sell memories in a marketplace monopolized by a powerful conglomerate.

Corrupt conglomerates. Very Jack.

Rich people buy skills, secrets, and experiences, and poor people sell their pasts to get by. Society is stratified not by wealth alone, but by people's memories.

I love the metaphor for capitalism's commodification of the Self!

The conglomerate hires the main character to extract a stolen military-grade memory from a client, only to discover it's a fragment from his own forgotten childhood. The memory is encrypted, and tampering with it triggers suppressed experiences. He discovers the company has been implanting synthetic memories to rewrite identities and influence political leaders. The main character's past is the prototype. He's not a victim; he was once the lead operative.

He stopped there? What kind of non-reader was his ex, anyway?

With a sigh, Alison sipped the last of her cold coffee. The world-building felt rough around the edges, expected for a first draft, but the core narrative was compelling.

She glanced at the clock, muttered a quiet curse, and slammed her cold coffee like a shot. Her morning had been devoured by Jack's manuscript.

I wonder if he was writing about societal gaslighting.

She attacked the thick layer of frost on her car windows as if the weather had targeted her personally. On her way to Lowe Mill, she couldn't imagine what kind of person would trash such an interesting book before Jack finished the first draft.

She must have been a small, jealous person. I'm jealous, but not jealous enough to kill a book.

Alison

Alison found Jack's truck in the parking lot, its windows fogged with condensation from sitting in the frosty morning air. He emerged as she opened her car door, releasing Bella from the back seat as she opened the hatch.

"You're late," he scolded, his breath misting. He lifted Bella when she jumped up to greet him, her long tail bobbing back and forth.

"I didn't expect you today. I was caught up in a riveting novel that you cruelly left unfinished." She pulled out her wagon, opening it with a snap.

"How could you have had time to see the email, let alone read the entire manuscript? I sent that late last night," he said, ignoring her compliment while avoiding Bella's tongue.

"I'm an early riser," she replied, dropping her bags into the wagon. It rattled behind her as they walked toward the elevator. Bella gave Jack air kisses as he cradled her in his arms. "Does your cat let you carry it all over the place like that?"

Jack chuckled. "Mac would never. He'd steal the chicken from your plate, but he's too proud to be cuddled unless it's his idea."

When they entered the elevator, Alison said, "You didn't have to say those nice things about my manuscript. I can handle the truth."

Jack scowled. "I try not to lie, Alison. If I thought your manuscript was bad, I wouldn't have said those things. I don't know what I would have told you, but I wouldn't make up praise for it."

Taken aback, Alison said, "I didn't mean to call you a liar. That level of honesty is unusual."

"In a man?"

"No, in a human. Women lie as often as men do. We're conditioned to be *nice*, no matter what. It's a survival skill. I also try to be honest. It isn't always easy, is it?" The elevator doors opened, and the wagon's rubber wheels thudded along the worn wooden hallway floor.

"You liked my book?" he asked.

"Of course, I did. I hated that you didn't finish it, though. You owe me the second half of that manuscript, Jack Morrison," she said, her keychain jangling as she found the correct key.

"You owe me the second half of yours. That novel is an intriguing suspense story. The romance part of it is great, but it's really the subplot, so I don't know whether you'll want to shop it around as a romance."

"Shop it around? Are you kidding? This was a passion project." She pulled her wagon to the office while Jack set Bella down, her tiny feet scrambling around her circuit of the store.

"Every novel should be a passion project." Jack followed Alison into the office to shed his jacket.

"I like that notion. What I don't like is someone beating up on my book, so I'm not sure I'm up for shopping it around to anyone." Alison positioned the wagon by the worktable and hung her wool coat on a hook. "We'll open the store, and then, if you don't mind, I'll have you sort through those speed dating lists to see who matched. Doing that kind of thing hurts my head, plus people's handwriting is terrible nowadays. I'll bet you a dollar that Melissa and Robb matched up."

"I'm not betting against that." Jack grabbed the short stack of lists and took them to the register stand to sort between customers.

Alison dragged the heavy sandwich board out the front door, gritting her teeth against the sonorous screech of wood against wood reverberating through the empty hallway. She carried Bella back to the office and dropped her behind the gate before joining her to wrap more book orders.

Five minutes later, a young woman rushed into the store, her wavy chestnut-colored hair pulled back into a messy ponytail. "Sorry I'm late, Alison. I had to scrape my car."

Alison shrugged. "It's fine, Brittany. Jack was the only one on time this morning."

"Jack?" Brittany's head swiveled, only then spotting him shuffling papers behind the counter.

"Jack Morrison is helping out until Valentine's Day. He's researching for a profile piece about the store."

"Jack Morrison from Alabama Online?" Brittany whispered. "Are you sure he's not doing a hit piece on you? He writes that *Love Is a Scam* column. I'd watch out for him, if I were you."

"Relax. I have nothing to hide from Jack Morrison. What would his hit piece say? He's already told me the worst that he can think of."

Brittany narrowed her eyes at Alison, suspicion hardening her gaze. "What did he say?"

Alison smirked. "Not much, just that I sell fantasies to delusional romantics and give them unrealistic expectations. If he printed that, it would still help business. Besides, Bella likes him."

"Bella, how could you?" Brittany's chin dipped, her lower lip jutting out in a comical pout as she expressed her disappointment over the dog's disloyalty. Bella responded with a doggy grin, her tail wagging as she waited for Brittany to fluff her ears. After obliging, Brittany grabbed her apron from its hook. "What does Jack's apron look like?"

"I don't have a man's apron, so he's apron-less. Besides, he won't be here that much longer, just three more weekends. Right now, he's sorting the speed dating sheets. He's been writing the blurbs and sending out the promotional announcements for the past few weeks."

"I wouldn't trust that curmudgeon with anything," Brittany muttered, tying her apron.

"He's not as bad as all that," Alison said.

"Why, thank you. I didn't know you still talked about me, Alison."

Alison didn't have to look. She would know that smooth voice anywhere, and it made her want to cringe.

"Brittany. How nice to see you," Quinn said, giving the young woman a warm smile as she nudged past him, ignoring his greeting. He sauntered through the gate and settled onto a stool at the worn work table. "I guess I'm not her type," he said with a smirk, his eyes lingering on the space where Brittany had been a moment before.

"She's barely out of her teens, Quinn. Control yourself."

"Isn't age gap romance a thing?" he asked, his finger tracing the edges of Alison's worn plastic tape dispenser.

"In books, it is. People like reading about dragons and trolls, too, but they wouldn't be happy to run into them in real life. Besides, you're still engaged, aren't you?"

"Yes, I'm still engaged. Are you still single?"

"Happily." Alison knew he intended the question as a barb, but his barbs were more like burrs under the saddle, an irritation, rather than a wound. "Tell me, please, why you want my copy of *Pride and Prejudice* so much that you're willing to take time out of your busy schedule to annoy me every weekend? You make enough money to replace it."

"It's a matter of principle, at this point," he said. "I want it back, and you won't give it to me."

"Funny, it's a matter of principle for me, too. It's mine, and you'll take nothing more from me, Quinn Walton." Taking a seat on the stool across from him, she could smell his cologne lingering in the air.

"I guess we're at an impasse, then. I have a secret, though." His eyes sparkled.

"What's that, now?" With a slight smile, Alison leaned on her forearms, entertained by the self-satisfied look on his face.

"I have the patience to wear you down. I always have." He said it tenderly, the way he used to, his touch gentle as he took her hand.

A shudder ran through her, and she recoiled. The touch lingered in a way that made her want to wash her hands. "You haven't changed one bit. I pity whoever marries you. Go take your fiancée out to lunch."

"I'm being dismissed so soon?" he asked, a hint of amusement in his voice as he stood to leave.

"You were never invited," Alison replied, nodding toward the baby gate.

After closing the gate behind himself, he turned to throw a dramatic gaze back into the office. "Remember," he called, "I won't give up, Alison."

She watched him leave, her shudder speaking volumes about her irritation. Quinn had never outgrown his high school drama club days. She wished he'd gone to Hollywood. The thought of him on screen, rather than in her life, made the idea of him far more appealing. The corner outside the shop swallowed him whole, and Alison's nerves settled as she resumed her work packing orders, the scent of cardboard boxes a welcome comfort.

Jack

It was Quinn, the same man from last Saturday, leaving after being rejected, a smile still on his face. He was well-heeled and well-groomed, and he treated Alison's shop like a second home, letting himself into the office like a welcome guest.

"Remember, I won't give up, Alison."

"What's with that Quinn guy?" Jack asked Brittany.

She regarded him through narrowed eyes for a moment, her lips a thin, tight line. "If you want to know Alison's business, you should ask *her*, not me."

Fair. No reason she'd trust me. Alison only hires women who can smell BS like gas leaks.

"What are you studying, Brittany?" he was still listing participants on a legal pad, trying to make his handwriting legible enough for Alison.

"Who told you I was in school?"

"It was a guess. I'm just trying to make conversation. I went to Alabama for Journalism."

"You need a journalism degree to write Love Is a Scam?" Brittany briskly shelved books from a cart.

"Ouch. No, you don't, but I'm doing what I can to make

ends meet while still sitting behind a keyboard." He printed Robb's name with the caution of a calligrapher and the skill of a third-grader.

She sighed. "Sorry, that was out of line. I'm studying Environmental Science and Communication. Do you always spend weeks working at businesses you're writing profiles about?"

"No, I owe Alison, and this is part of an agreement we came to." Jack worked on the next name, wishing he had some graph paper to make his job easier.

"Are you serious right now? What did you owe her, like $600?"

"What do you mean?"

Brittany set the books she was shelving back on the cart and stood near the register so Jack could hear her speak under her breath. "Alison can't afford to pay much more than minimum wage and an employee discount, and you're pretty much useless, if she's having you do busy work like that. If you owed her anything more, you basically robbed her blind. That store profile had better be *golden*."

"Or what?" Jack asked, amused by the young woman's threatening disposition.

"You know what it is to be canceled, right?"

"My generation invented canceling," Jack replied.

"So you know how it works. Good. I'm studying Communication. I know how it works, too. You write a glowing profile about this delightful bookstore and its lovely owner, or you'll *wish* you had a job doing *anything*."

"Why are you all so *hostile*?" Jack shuffled some more papers around. "You know, this task would be easier in a spreadsheet."

"Are you seriously having trouble with this, Jack? Put men down the side, women across the top. Slash for yes, slash the other way for yes-back. X means match. Sixth-grade stuff."

Jack blinked at Brittany. "Thanks," he said. "I was distracted, and you made it much easier."

"It's all that new math everybody cried about," Brittany said, returning to her cart. "I might not be so hostile if you didn't base your career on destroying businesses like Alison's. And, you know, it would be easier for you to concentrate if you took your nose out of her personal business."

"I go after businesses that swindle people, not independent booksellers. I just wondered who that guy Quinn thought he was, walking in here like he owns the place."

"You want to know who he *thinks* he is? I'll tell you. Quinn *thinks* he's a snacc, but he just gives me the icks."

Jack raised an eyebrow at her. "I refuse to believe those words came out of your mouth."

"They don't usually, but it's fun to watch you translate in your head." Brittany offered him a genuine smile. "Mind your own business, Jack. I don't know how much you owe Alison, but you should be grateful for the sweet deal she gave you. When you write that profile, be extra nice, because she's an extra nice lady…and I'm not."

"I will remember that," he said, continuing to record matches.

That guy couldn't be interested in buying the store, so what does he want?

Jack

On his way home, Jack called Robb, turning the heater fan down so he could hear.

"Did you find out?" Robb asked.

"Hi, I'm fine. How about you?" Jack replied, his voice sharp. "Yes, you matched with Melissa. You'll get an email with the information."

"Are we jealous? Maybe if you stepped up your game, you could get a date, too, once in a while," Robb taunted. "Did you tell Alison about liking her manuscript?"

"I sent her an email last night, along with my manuscript. She read it this morning and was almost late for opening the store because she had to finish it. She wants the rest, which I do not have, because my soul was crushed." Jack navigated through the 7:30 pm Saturday traffic.

"I told you," Robb said. "Everyone except for She Who Will Not Be Named has wants the end of that book. You liked Alison's work, and she thought yours was good. She doesn't even like your column, so you can't say she's a fan."

"Apparently, I don't have fans; I have hate readers. I'm

not sure how I feel about that. There's something going on with Alison, though. That same guy who came through last Saturday? He showed up again, walking into the back office like he owned the place, and saying, 'Remember, Alison, I won't give up,' as he left. When I asked the college girl who was working there about him, she said to ask Alison or mind my own business."

"Listen to the college girl. Like I said last week, he probably wants to buy her out."

Jack sighed, gripping the wheel harder. "She works too hard for not enough money for anyone to try buying her out."

"Maybe she has some real estate he wants," Robb said.

"She rents," Jack said.

Robb sent a frustrated growl over the phone. "You want a story, Jack? The guy is madly in love with her, and he's proposing, but she keeps turning him down. Still, he won't let go, and that's why nobody tells you what's going on. That's why he leaves tossing some dramatic 'I won't give up' nonsense over his shoulder."

"Do you think so?" Jack asked, hearing a strange anxiousness in his voice and feeling an odd stab of regret for…

For what?

"No, you dolt. You've inhaled too much bookstore air. If you're that worried about someone else marrying Alison, you should ask her out."

Jack pulled up to the gate outside his apartment complex, taking out his key card. "You're missing the point, Robb."

"I think you're the one missing the point, Jack. It's okay to like her. She's not your real boss, you know."

"Why do you keep insisting I like her?" The gate rolled open, and Jack drove to his building. "I've gotta go. I'm home now. You know, I didn't even have to go in today. I went in for you, and in return I get threatened by a literal teenager—okay, fine, a twenty-year-old with murder in her eyes—and you repay me like this."

"Wait, before you go, I have something important to tell you," Robb said.

"Yeah?" Jack parked his truck in front of his building, leaving it running to keep the phone connection.

"I know tomorrow is your laundry day. Take hangers to the laundromat. Hang and fold your laundry as it comes out of the dryer so you don't walk around looking like a bum."

"Thanks, Mom," Jack replied, ending the call.

CHAPTER ELEVEN
Captain

Wednesday, January 25

Jack

The Wednesday morning meeting in the parking lot left Jack speechless. Sure, he knew the weekend's theme was pirate romances, after the singles' book club selection, *Plundering Seas,* but the sight of Alison in a pirate queen costume, stepping from her car, made his heart pound.

The character of Isobel Hartwell was Jack's first movie crush, and Alison had brought her to life. Alison, sporting a leather hat and corset worn over a peasant blouse and long vest, took his breath away. Her unbound hair cascaded around her arms, the strands partially hiding a leather baldric containing a plastic pirate's flintlock pistol and a knife. She finished her outfit with worn leather pantaloons and sturdy, cuffed boots. She was Isobel, wearing Alison's glasses.

"It's pretty silly, isn't it?" Alison pushed her glasses up

the bridge of her nose and opened the back car door for Bella to jump out. She had tied a red bandana around the dog's neck.

"No," was all Jack could choke out, his hand brushing lightly against hers as he took Bella's leash.

Does her perfume smell like spiced rum? That would be unfair.

"Well, don't worry. I remembered how much you hated wearing the kilt, so I'm not making you wear a costume."

The disappointment hit Jack like a physical blow. "I'd be your Elias Drake," he mumbled.

Alison opened her car's hatch, then turned to raise an eyebrow at him.

Suddenly, he understood what he had said. "I mean, I would wear an Elias Drake costume."

"Really?" she asked, voice tinged with skepticism as she placed her hands on her hips, just below the corset.

After a moment, he realized she expected an answer, and his eyes, which had been captivated by her hands, lifted to meet hers. "Uh, yeah. *Plundering Seas* was my favorite movie growing up."

"I guess it's a good thing I rented a Captain Elias Drake costume, just in case," she replied with a mischievous grin. She hefted the wagon from the car and snapped it open without a thought.

"You *were* planning to make me dress up again?" Jack's disappointment turned to something between irritation and joy, two emotions he didn't know could coexist.

"Nope." She pulled the costume from the car, the plastic garment bag rustling in her hands, then grabbed an extra cardboard box from the hatch. "I wasn't even going to ask you. It was only for if you volunteered." She looked up, and he had to avert his gaze from her bare shoulder, where goosebumps rose on her skin in the crisp morning air. "And you did, but I won't hold you to it, if you change your mind."

"I—no, it's good," he stammered, voice cracking like a teenager's. "Are you cold? Do you need my coat?"

"I don't think a coat will fit over this mess, but thanks. I only have to make it to the elevator. We pirates are a tough lot, after all. Are you coming?" Alison had walked ahead of him while he stood in a stupor. When she looked over her shoulder to call back to him, he found his lungs wouldn't expand enough to take in the air he needed. He'd follow her anywhere.

Get it together. It's Alison, not Isobel. Stop being weird.

With Bella at his side, Jack trotted to catch up. His breath frosted in the frigid air, and he hoped the cold would clear his head.

Once they were in the store, Alison handed the pirate's shirt, vest, and pants to Jack. "You can add the rest when you get back here. No use carrying all this stuff to the bathroom. There's so much, I'm glad I had the wagon to carry it up."

He removed his jacket and handed it to her in exchange, and she regarded him as if something was out of place. "You seem very...put together today. Is that a new outfit?"

"No." He wouldn't admit to following Robb's advice and hanging his clothes up fresh from the dryer to prevent wrinkles.

"Well, you look nice." Alison smiled as she turned to walk toward the office, and Jack had to remind himself to leave.

For crying out loud. It's Alison, the book nerd. Go put your pirate costume on and act like an adult.

Jack

Jack didn't look like much of a pirate wearing just the shirt, vest, and short pants, but he returned to the store, ready to trade his shoes for pirate boots.

"This is a lot of pieces." Alison gestured toward the haphazard pile of costume accessories on the table. "They sent me a picture as a guide."

Jack didn't need a picture, but he was too embarrassed to say so. Since he was twelve, the image of Captain Elias Drake, the swashbuckling pirate with a piercing gaze, had lived rent-free in his head. He knew where every costume piece belonged.

"Boots first." Alison handed him a pair of heavy, wide-cuffed leather boots, much like her own.

"Now, two belts with ridiculously oversized buckles, for your pistols."

Alison's gaze wracked Jack's nerves as he adjusted the belts, the weight of her scrutiny almost as heavy as the pirate coat she then handed to him.

"Your baldric, Captain Drake." She handed him the distressed leather harness after he'd finished shrugging on the long coat.

Don't call me Captain Drake. I'm already halfway to emotional puberty over here.

"Thanks." A weak smile tugged at his lips as he fumbled with the baldric.

She rewarded him with a smirk, the corner of her lip curling upwards, then cocked her head to the side. "You didn't tie the belt ends. They're all loose."

He knew they had to be tied. She was distracting him.

I would be fine if she would let me finish by myself.

Alison released an impatient little sigh as he fumbled with the loose leather straps. "You're doing it wrong. Here, I'll help." She knotted the belt ends near the buckle before he could protest. Her nimble fingers brushing against his abdomen were nearly his undoing. She stepped back with a quick nod of approval. "There, that's better. Here are your weapons."

With a flourish, she handed him an arsenal of plastic weapons, making sure he tucked each in its proper place. Then she held his tricorn hat before him like a bishop presenting a new king with his crown.

"And, finally, your hat, Captain Drake." Alison placed it in his waiting hands.

A nervous swallow escaped Jack's lips as he settled the hat on his head while Alison stepped back, her eyes shining with delight, to appreciate his costume.

"Hold on." She reached up and adjusted his coat collar. Her fingers brushed his neck, sending shivers down his spine. "You look great!" she exclaimed with a pleased expression as she returned her hands to her hips.

"You, too," he croaked.

Alison frowned when her phone alarm sounded. "We've spent so much time dressing you that we haven't prepared the store. Good thing Wednesday mornings are dead, right?"

"Yeah," he said, his gaze following her brisk walk to the front as he bent to scratch Bella's ears.

She has no idea she just emotionally waterboarded me.

The shuddering screech of Alison dragging the sandwich board against the wooden floors made Jack's teeth itch. He organized a display of books depicting women as dark-eyed pirate queens and captains, or as ravishing captives. All were set against raging ocean battles and ruby sunsets.

The front display, however, featured the bookstore's main attraction for the next two weeks. Several copies of *Plundering Seas* awaited arrangement. A sign listed the singles' book club and a movie screening in Lowe Mill's theater with a shadow cast the following week.

"A shadow cast?" Jack asked, adjusting the sign.

"Yeah, you know. People who act out the movie in front of the screen. They do it every year. I certainly can't afford to purchase screening rights for that film."

"And I didn't know?" he asked, his brow furrowed. "I live, like, two miles away."

"You should get out more, Captain." Her vest billowed behind her like a silken sail as she strode off to set up another display. Jack was torn between asking her to stop calling him "Captain" and begging her to do it again. Instead, he responded with a quote from the movie. "Remind me never to get between you and your rum."

Alison stopped, a giggle bubbling up in her chest that made him feel giddy. "I love that scene, the one where she knocks out the bounty hunter with her tankard." She arranged her display, offering a quote of her own. "Do you flirt with all your prisoners, Captain?"

The curve of her bare shoulder was visible as she looked back at him. A smile played on her lips, and Jack decided she could call him "Captain" for the next two weeks, maybe longer. He gave her his best Elias Drake impression. "Only the ones who threaten to stab me in my sleep."

Jack

Jack had survived bagpipes, but sea shanties were a war crime. Alison endured them for an hour before admitting she couldn't take it and switching to her regular mix. After some discussion, they draped her pirate flag behind the corner of the front window — recognizable, but not blocking customers' view of the store's interior.

Jack didn't fully realize until he set up the display that he had two weeks ahead of ignoring Alison in her Isobel costume. Alison, fortunately, spent much of the afternoon packing orders.

I'll get used to it.

As he swept the floor near the store's front door, the unmistakable sound of someone fangirling accosted Jack.

"Captain Drake!" a woman gushed. "Look, Grace! It's Captain Drake!" The woman, her blond, curly hair left loose about her chin, had a four-year-old girl by the hand.

Jack, doubtful of the girl's willingness to engage with a heavily armed pirate, crouched where he was. He reached into his childhood to imagine the most comforting thing he could and tried to channel Steve from Blues Clues. Despite giving the child a finger-waggling wave, she hid behind her mother, chanting, "No."

"But, Honey, you love Captain Drake," she said.

Mom was the actual fan here. Jack didn't blame the girl a bit.

"Don't you want to say hi? Maybe Captain Drake will let me take a picture of you with him."

"Mama, no. Pirates are scary," Grace said.

"It's okay, Grace," Jack said, trying to let the child off the hook. "I used to be afraid of pirates, too. We can be scary. You don't have to come near me."

Mom gave Jack a secret scowl.

"Captain, are you scaring the lass?" Alison's voice came from behind.

"Isobel!" the girl cried. "Mama, Isobel!"

Alison greeted the girl, who dragged her mother past Jack to reach her hero.

"How are ye, Lassie?" Alison asked, crouching down to Grace's level. "*Can she have chocolate?*" she mouthed to the girl's mother, who nodded. "I have some treasure for ye," Alison said, handing over a chocolate coin wrapped in gold foil.

The girl accepted the candy, delighted. "Thank you. I'm Grace. Are you scared of Captain Drake?"

"I was when I first met him, but not any more. Now, I'm a pirate, too! We go on adventures together."

"You're pretty, Isobel," Grace said, fingering the gold chain around Alison's neck.

Yes, you are *pretty, Isobel.*

"Why, thank ye, Lassie," Alison replied. "Yer pretty as a picture, yerself."

"Can I have a picture?" Mom asked.

"Of course! Grace, if I protect you, will you let Captain

Drake be in the picture, too?"

Grace considered Alison's question, her eyes wide and her mouth puckered in thought, then nodded. "Will you hold my hand?"

Mom nodded at Alison.

"Okay, Grace. I'll hold your hand. Is it okay for Captain Drake to come close for the picture, now?"

Jack felt the child's disapproval in her bright blue eyes. Apparently, only girl pirates were acceptable. "Okay. No touching."

"Of course not!" Jack said, ready to run from the store at the accusation. "No touching at all!" He edged in beside Alison.

"Closer," Mom said.

This would be Jack's next two weeks, so he had to get used to it or die trying. He edged closer to Alison.

Her perfume does *smell like spiced rum.*

"Smile!"

After a few pictures with Grace, Mom wanted some with just Jack and Alison. "You two are adorable! Come on, pretend you like each other."

Jack's soul attempted to leave his body through his left ear.

Alison drew one of her plastic blades, holding it against his neck as she grabbed his lapel with a wicked grin.

"Who needs rescuing when I've got a blade and a sharp tongue?" she drawled, her face near his.

He put one hand on her waist and held the other up in surrender, like in the movie.

"Perfect! Give me your card so I can send you the picture."

"Sure. Come on back. We have the original *Plundering*

Seas book and the one written by the actor who played Captain Drake. They're both fun reads. And don't forget the costumed movie screening next weekend."

"I haven't read either book. Let me pick those up while I'm here. You two are so cute together, and you've been such good sports."

Alison flitted off to the register, leaving Jack listening to his pulse thumping behind his ears. Luckily, she hadn't a clue what was going on in his head. If she ever found out, he'd have to fake his own death.

CHAPTER TWELVE

Part of the Deal

Friday, January 27

Jack

The costumes were a problem. Every time Jack caught sight of Alison's leather-and-lace Isobel getup, he forgot how to breathe. Meanwhile, customers just kept buying books.

As he stood in the store Friday afternoon, Jack received a message from Alison containing the photo taken two days before. He would never look that much like Captain Elias Drake again, and there he was, posing with Isobel.

Alison.

He zoomed in on their faces, and he couldn't get over how much it looked like she was enjoying herself. Jack could still feel his hand on Alison's waist.

Something nudged the center of his back, making him jump. "You kidnapped me. The least you could do is stop looking so handsome while doing it." Another movie line.

Alison had approached him from behind, holding him at plastic gunpoint.

How could she be quiet in those pirate boots?

"If you two flirt any harder, the ship's going to sink from sheer tension." Jack and Alison both swiveled their heads to see who was joining in the movie quotes.

"Melissa!" Alison lowered her gun. "How do you like us?" She spread her arms to show off her costume, but Melissa directed her attention to Jack.

"If it isn't Jack Morrison, dressed up as Captain Elias Drake," she said with a smile. "I didn't know you had a fun bone in your body."

Alison coughed to cover a giggle.

Jack rolled his eyes. "You have the mind of a twelve-year-old, Alison. Melissa, I'll have you know that I am lots of fun."

Melissa shook her head at him. "I have seen no evidence of this. Prove it."

Jack put his arms around Alison, drawing her close and giving her his best Captain Drake impression. "You steal breath better than I steal gold. And I'm *very* good at stealing gold."

Alison raised her chin at him to reply in a haughty voice. "You think a wink and a waistcoat make you irresistible?"

"Add in charm and a cutlass, and most people agree," Jack replied into her ear.

"I stand corrected," Melissa said. "You two are having too much fun. I need pictures."

"Who are you going to dress up as for the screening next Saturday?" Alison asked.

"First Mate Quinn, of course," Melissa said. "She's a riot."

"You're dressing up?" Jack asked.

"Of course I am. Everyone does. You're lucky Alison rented that costume early. Otherwise, you would have been stuck piecing something together from your closet instead of wearing the most incredible Captain Drake outfit I've seen off-screen. My girl does not skimp on the costumes. The Mill is dead right now. Let's set up for book club, and then you two can do *all* the poses for me."

After setting up, Melissa did, in fact, have them do all the poses. Jack silently begged the pirate gods that Alison would forward those pictures, too.

Melissa led the book club in a lively discussion of how the book differed from the movie. They debated its commentary on unhealthy gender stereotypes in its satire of pirate fantasy tropes.

Jack and Alison worked in the background. He leaned close to her and whispered, "I thought it was a fun family movie."

"It is. The book is just as much fun, but it has much more to digest. Same story, different animal. They haven't even touched on the arbitrary nature of love as it's depicted in the book, or the use of the superior in character arcs."

Jack took a moment to process what Alison had said. "You said you only took business writing courses. That's some pretty involved literary analysis there. You don't pick that up on the street."

Alison chuckled. "You make it sound like attending community college means I grew up as a waif in the streets of nineteenth century London. This isn't Charles Dickens. I graduated from high school, and I have the Internet. The entire collection of human knowledge is there for the picking, Jack. We readers like learning."

"I didn't mean it that way. I meant that…well, someone has to teach you what you don't know."

"Ah, The Dunning-Kruger effect." She offered a slow nod. "People watch a documentary and think they're shark experts. My mama taught me well, though, along with a couple of dedicated high school English teachers, who covered overcoming cognitive bias."

"Is that why you hate read me? To overcome cognitive bias?"

Alison straightened her glasses. "Who said I hate read you?"

"You did. You asked how you could hate read me if you kept agreeing with me."

She flushed, and it was absolutely adorable. "I suppose I did. That was unkind of me. I agree with you fairly often, but the way you phrase it can be…"

Jack waited for her to find the word.

"You're not going to finish my sentence for me?" she asked, cocking her head.

"Why would you talk if I knew what you would say? I hate when people do that, especially people who don't know me that well, yet. I still want to hear the end of that sentence."

"…difficult to swallow."

Jack stifled a laugh with an awkward snort. "I'm glad I waited for that. There's no way I could have guessed that phrase in a hundred years."

"Now who has the mind of a twelve-year-old?"

Jack's ears grew hot. "I mean, Alison, that I can never predict when you'll be an intimidatingly direct business woman, or an intimidatingly proper southern lady."

"Oh, that southern lady nonsense is my Gran's doing.

She tried to make me into a proper lady. The manners are helpful, but the rest is a nuisance Mama tried to stamp out. Some of it stuck, and other parts…I trot them out for fun, occasionally. I hope you realize there's more to me than those two sides. To paraphrase a great philosopher, women are like onions."

"Indeed. This week I've learned that you're also an intimidating pirate queen. What did your mother do?"

"*Does.* She's an engineer. What else would she be in this town?"

"Maybe a journalist or a romance bookstore owner," he replied, "but you're right: chances are, in this town, she would be an engineer. How does she feel about your store?"

Alison shrugged. "Supportive, but ultimately uninterested. She likes cozy mysteries, and she doesn't believe in happy endings."

The book club members stood to leave, their chairs rattling as they maneuvered their way out of the circular chair arrangement. Melissa left to retrieve the chair cart.

"We've got this, Jack, if you want to change into your street clothes. That outfit is a heck of a job." Alison began folding chairs and stacking them against the wall so she could move the display tables back into place. "We'll reset the displays in the morning."

Jack removed everything but the costume base in the office, then walked to the bathroom to change the rest of the way, watching other studios close for the night. They left, Alison in full Isobel regalia, Melissa leading Bella, him clutching his new book—hoping the cold air would slap some sense into him. It didn't.

Jack

When Jack returned home, Mac sniffed the book, then meowed and sat on it until Jack refilled his kibble and water bowls. Jack sank into the couch, eating a microwaved frozen breakfast sandwich while he read, until his phone rang.

Jack picked up Robb's call. "Hey, what's up?"

"Just wanted to know if you had fun playing pirates again today."

"Better than being sued," Jack said, proud of the casual tone of his voice. He tipped up his can of Dr. Pepper.

"I'm sure it is, especially since you've had the hots for Isobel since you were a kid."

"How would you know?" Jack set his phone on the arm of the couch to wave Mac away from his sandwich.

"Because you've told me…repeatedly. Cute little book nerd Alison in an Isobel costume? Bet you can't keep your hands off her. When will you ask her out?"

"For crying out loud, Robb. It's Alison. Do you think I just fall apart for any woman in a pirate costume?" His brain replayed every stupid moment he'd wrapped an arm around her waist.

Great. Now I'm embarrassing myself retroactively.

"I don't know. Did Mindy ever dress up as Isobel for you?"

Now he's just pushing my buttons.

"Mindy didn't wear costumes. At most she'd find some headband to wear because she didn't want to look silly. She also hated *Plundering Seas*. She said it was for children." Jack took a bite of his sandwich, hoping to save himself from the cat, who loomed over him from the sofa arm like a vulture.

"And you went right along with her, didn't you?" Robb asked.

"Maybe it was time for me to grow up," Jack said. "We don't all make a living running around in costumes every weekend."

"Growing up is taking care of yourself, not giving up on things you love. Mac eats better than you do."

"Of course he eats well. I'm a good cat dad." Jack shoved the last piece of sandwich into his mouth and showed Mac his empty hands.

"You're telling me you care more about the cat than you do about yourself. Do yourself a favor: get a decent haircut and find a recipe to cook. Something with vegetables."

"Did you have any other life advice for me?" Jack winced as Mac stepped onto his lap, concentrating all his eighteen pounds on four paws until he stretched himself out over the length of Jack's legs.

"I wanted to know what you thought about my asking Melissa to attend the movie with me next weekend," Robb said. "It's an unusual first date choice, but she seems to attend most of Alison's events."

"She's already going as First Mate Quinn, but she didn't

mention a date. I've been told costumes can be hard to come by last minute. If you plan to go, you should find one early."

"Thanks for the tip. See you there?"

"It's part of the deal," Jack said, trying to sound like he wasn't looking forward to it.

CHAPTER THIRTEEN

This You?

Saturday, January 28

Jack

The store was even busier on Saturday, with groups of passers-by drawn in by Jack and Alison's costumes. Several new customers purchased gift certificates and books as Valentine's Day gifts.

"I'm sure you hate this, since you think Valentine's Day is a scam," Alison said after another customer left with a gift, "but this is one of my best times of the year, besides Christmas."

"You have other best times of the year?"

"Summer beach read season is pretty good," she said.

"Is there a beach around here?" Jack asked, grabbing the feather duster.

"Not a real one." Monique, dressed as the villain Captain Josephina Martin, shelved books until the next customer could arrive.

"Then why is there a beach *season*?"

"Because people want to imagine their life isn't a fluorescent-lit cubicle," Monique said. "Let them have the fantasy. What is your problem with happy endings, anyway, Jack?"

"They're unrealistic." He whisked the tops of the immaculate bookcases.

"Says the man who writes Science Fiction," Alison retorted. "I've never had a happy ending in real life, but I sure love to imagine they can happen, the way you like to imagine being an astronaut and fixing the doohickey to save the space mission."

Doesn't everyone like imagining that?

"Or being the dashing, irresistible pirate. You can't even *pretend* you're not having fun in that Elias Drake costume," Monique said. "No wonder your column reads like a tax audit. You only have fun when someone stuffs you into a costume and shoves you onto a stage."

"Oh my gosh!" a woman called from the door. "Everyone is dressed up. Is the movie tonight?"

"Nope," Monique said, switching into sales mode. "We're celebrating the books this week, along with all pirate romance."

As Monique helped the customer, Jack thought about the words people used to describe him and his column: no fun, vindictive, destructive, dour. A ten-pound weight settled on his chest, and he struggled not to groan.

It's no wonder Mindy left me at the altar.

He texted Robb.

> **Jack**: Am I dour?
> **Robb:** Depends.

Jack: What do you mean, depends? Either
I'm dour, or I'm not.
Robb: Look at the name of your column,
buddy.
Jack: So you're saying I'm dour.
Robb: You could stand to have more fun.
Jack: I have lots of fun.
Robb: When was the last time you had fun?
Jack: Yesterday. Melissa took pictures of
Isobel and me goofing around in our
Plundering Seas costumes.
Robb: ...Who?
Jack: Alison.
Robb: ...
Jack: Don't start. Just answer.
Robb: ASK. HER. OUT.

"Captain!" Alison called.

Jack's stomach flipped.

"What are you doing on your phone? It's picture time," she said, waving him over.

He stood beside Alison, grasping her waist as they squeezed in together for the photo, their hats knocking into each other.

"Okay, now just you two," the customer said, stepping back. "Look at each other."

On a whim, Jack swept Alison into his arms, catching her off guard. She gasped, her lips slightly parted. Their eyes met, and heat jolted between them, freezing them both. It wasn't Isobel he was holding; it was Alison. From far away, the customer's voice filtered through, overcoming Jack's pounding heart. "Perfect. Can I post this? I'll tag the store."

Jack released Alison, who adjusted her glasses and smiled. "It's fine with me. Captain?"

"Sure," Jack said, using his best Elias Drake impression to keep his voice from cracking. "Anything to please the ladies."

Monique stifled a laugh.

We'll see who's dour.

Jack drew his cutlass and charged at Monique. "Silence, you villainous wretch!"

Monique drew a rapier, which looked more like a cheap lightsaber toy. "No *man* silences Captain Josephina Martin!"

"Hey! No sword fights in the bookstore, or I'll keelhaul you both," Alison called, her eyes sparkling with amusement.

Monique chuckled as she re-sheathed her rapier. "Aw, Mom. You're no fun."

See? Made you smile. I'm not so dour after all.

Alison

Alison returned to the register, where she took a long sip from her giant insulated cup, waiting for her heart rate to slow back to normal.

Well, that *came out of nowhere. I probably just imagined it.*

Near closing time, Alison asked Jack if he wanted to go change.

"I'll just wear the costume home and clean it up before next week," he said. "That way, I can be dressed before I arrive on Wednesday."

"If you want. It's a lot to keep track of," Alison said. "Take the accessories box with you."

"I'll manage," he said.

"If you two have this under control, do you mind if I take off? They want me to work tonight, and the extra time would help," Monique said.

Alison waved her off. After they finished closing up for the week, she handed Bella's leash to Jack. They strolled across the parking lot together, the wagon rattling behind. Jack seemed like he wanted to say something, so after loading her car, Alison stood in the cold while he stared at her like a man holding a sentence hostage.

"Thanks for renting my costume," he finally said. "This week was more fun than I've had in a long time."

"You must be hurting for fun, if forced labor is your preferred entertainment."

He tucked his chin and gave her a tender look. "It didn't feel like forced labor."

She tried to ignore the flutter in her stomach, in case she was imagining things. "In that case, thank you. You've been a great sport about the pictures. Who knows what people will say when they find photos of Jack Morrison having fun in a romance bookstore all over social media? It could ruin your reputation."

"From what I've been hearing, my reputation could use a little ruin."

The silence that followed felt like it stretched long enough to fossilize her.

"Well, it's cold out here," Alison said with a smile as she stepped around Jack to reach her car door. "I should get going. Dinner calls."

"Yeah. Dinner," he said, drawn from his stupor as Alison took Bella's leash and encouraged her into the car. "I'll, uh, see you Wednesday."

"Only if you want," she reminded him, stepping into her car.

"Wouldn't want to waste your costume rental."

She smirked at the unconvincing argument. "Okay, Wednesday it is. Have a good week."

"Uh-huh," he replied, giving her an odd look as she closed the car door.

Melissa pinged Alison's phone with the words, "This you?" accompanied by the customer's photo of Alison and Jack, sharing a smoldering look.

Alison felt that rush of electricity again. Maybe she hadn't imagined it. Unsure how to respond, she replied with a thumbs up. Her phone rang.

"If he didn't kiss you after that picture, the man needs to be checked for a pulse." Melissa said.

"It was just a picture," Alison said, starting her car and pulling out of the parking lot.

"That was *not* just a picture. That was chemistry. He also couldn't keep his hands off you during our photo session yesterday. Looks like Mr. Love is a Scam has a thing for you."

"Ha. Nobody has a thing for me. Jack just has a thing for Isobel Hartwell and nostalgia."

"I'm not so sure about that," Melissa said. "He's there all the time, whether you want him or not. By the way, his buddy Robb asked me to go with him to the screening next week."

"Is he dressing up?" Alison asked.

"I told him I was. If he doesn't, he's a stick in the mud," Melissa said.

"Stick in the mud or not, he's a good-looking guy."

"So is Quinn."

"Ugh. Good point," Alison said. "Meet you for brunch at the Standard tomorrow?"

"That's why I called. I just wanted the scoop on you and Jack first."

"No scoop. Just Jack having fun playing pirates. Tell Robb to clue Jack's next girlfriend in so she can buy some costumes for them."

Alison thought about the photo for the rest of the drive home.

Who was Jack looking at? Was it me, or was it Isobel?

After shedding the costume accessories, she took Bella for her last walk of the day, passing all the little cottages. Some had Christmas lights still adorning their porches, while others sported Valentine's Day decorations. Bella stopped here and there for a sniff, sometimes eyeing the occasional lifelike decoration with suspicion.

Alison encouraged the little dog with a light tug of the leash, knowing a grocery store salad waited at home, and knowing—unfortunately—that the photo would be waiting in her brain the whole night, too.

CHAPTER FOURTEEN

Tomorrow

Saturday, February 4

Alison

"Don't let it go to your head," Brittany called from behind the register after another customer took Jack's picture with Alison.

He rolled his eyes. "No chance of that, I'm afraid. I have plenty of reminders when I wear street clothes."

"Nice haircut, though," Brittany said. "Suits you."

"Thanks." Jack scratched the back of his freshly clipped neck.

"I agree," Alison said, pushing her glasses up from the end of her nose. "It does suit you." She shelved some books from her cart before heading back to the office.

It seemed criminally unfair that a pirate promotion, of all things, suited Jack better than real life ever had. He appeared to have fun wearing the costume, posing for photos, and even joking with Brittany and Monique.

Dozens of customer photos of Jack and Alison were floating around social media, tagged with #HappilyEverAfterBooks, and business had been much better than usual. He wasn't the same bitter man she had met just a few weeks before.

And all it took was a pirate costume.

When he took some books from the cart to help her shelve, Alison said, "I'd never have guessed you would enjoy this promotion so much, Jack. You seemed to be above all this."

"My ex was embarrassed when I acted goofy. She said that things like this were childish. In fact, she hated *Plundering Seas*, saying I should have outgrown it a decade ago. I loved her, so I thought maybe she was right."

"Is that why you broke up?" Alison asked. "Because she was afraid of looking silly?"

"No. We were days away from getting married when she broke off the engagement. Practically left me at the altar. I didn't even know anything was wrong, which is on me. She made it pretty clear how embarrassing I was after she left, though."

I never thought I would empathize with Jack Morrison. The weight of it sank into her chest.

"Some people are good at hiding how they feel," Alison said. "Just because you didn't suspect your fiancée was unhappy while you were in the middle of getting your tux fitted doesn't mean it was all your fault. If she was embarrassed to be with you, she didn't deserve you. You dodged a bullet."

"A canceled wedding is a pretty expensive bullet to dodge, especially when you're still paying off student loans. That's why I didn't have the money to pay you for the book I ruined. I didn't actually think that you were lying about the value. I just didn't want to believe it, myself."

"If I had an extra $2200 lying around, it might not have been such a big deal to me, either," Alison said, straightening a shelf full of books.

Jack cast her a skeptical glance, and she pursed her lips, reconsidering her statement. "No, you're right. I would have thrown a fit, regardless, but what's done is done. It was an accident."

Jack pressed his lips together, nodding. "Yeah, it was. I *am* sorry."

"It's—"

"Ali. Still playing pirates? How *cute*."

Alison tightened her grip on the novel in her hand until her fingers turned white. She closed her eyes to take a calming breath as she fought the urge to ruin a perfectly good book by throwing it at the man behind her. Did Quinn think she'd hide if he didn't sneak up on her? She never had, but the idea was something to consider.

"Quinn Walton," she said, turning to face him, "Can't you see I'm busy?"

He must have been on his way out for the evening again. She had a brief fantasy of strangling him with his silk tie and burying him in his black woolen dress coat. Of course, she might get away with accidentally scuffing up his perfect black dress shoes with her pirate boots. She guessed that his dark hair, tousled from the wind, was how he wanted it to look, too. The man never had an unplanned moment.

He gifted Alison with a condescending smile, making her feel small for a moment as he appraised Jack's and her appearance.

"Jack Morrison." Jack offered his hand, and she fought off a second of queasiness.

These two becoming friends was the last thing I needed.

At the sound of Jack's name, Quinn's expression slipped for a moment, then found its place again as he took his hand. "The Alabama Online guy?"

"One and the same," Jack said.

Alison watched a strange mutual curiosity pass between the two men as they shook hands. Quinn's eyes shifted between Jack and her as if performing some sort of mental calculus. It seemed uncharacteristically unrehearsed for Quinn.

"I can see you're busy here. I'll speak with you later," Quinn said, nodding to Alison. "Good to finally meet you, Jack," he said before walking to the register.

Alison watched him speak with a reluctant Brittany for a moment before writing something on a card and handing it to her. He hurried from the store without looking back, his dress shoes briskly clicking against the wood floor. Brittany seemed as puzzled as Alison and Jack as they watched him walk away.

"What was that about?" Jack asked.

"I couldn't say," Alison said. "He's never acted like that before. And what was that about finally meeting you?"

"I don't know. I've only ever seen him here."

Alison studied Brittany again, who read something on her phone, then put it in her pocket, casting a suspicious glance at Jack.

What on earth did Quinn say to Brittany?

As they closed the shop a short time later, Alison asked Jack to join her for dinner before the screening. "I'm in the mood for barbecue. Have you had Kar's Char yet?" She sought Bella out of habit, despite knowing she had left her dog at home for the day.

"Not for a while. That sounds great," he replied. "Brittany, you joining us?"

"I'll pass." She looked and sounded as if Jack had offered her a plate of week-old shellfish.

"Did I say something?" Jack asked Alison as their steps echoed down the deserted hallway to the restaurant on the other end of the mill.

"I don't think so," she said. "As usual, things got weird when Quinn showed up. I'm sure it had nothing to do with you."

Jack took his chance to test the waters. "I know it's none of my business, but—"

"You're right," Alison interrupted, "but I'll tell you anyway. Quinn is my ex. He wants something of mine, and I refuse to give it to him. Still, being the most irritating man alive, he insists on showing up to ask for it until I give in."

"I thought I was the most irritating man alive," Jack joked.

"Not even close," Alison said. "You're not the only one with a terrible ex story, either. Quinn and I were together for three years. He kept hinting that he *would* propose, saying I was in danger of turning him into the marrying type. It turned out he was cheating on me the whole time, and now he's engaged to someone else, less than a year after we split. So, yes, he wanted to get married, just not to me."

"Would it help if I told you I think he's a smarmy creep who isn't worth your time?" Jack asked.

"It's nothing I haven't thought or heard before, but the validation is always helpful," Alison said. "I don't still love him. Sometimes I just feel like, during the time I wasted with him, I might have missed my own chance at love while he was finding his behind my back. It hurts to know that I was just a placeholder. To him, I was a bookmark, not a story."

As their footsteps echoed off the brick walls of the empty connector space between the two buildings, Jack took Alison's hand. "Wait," he said, stopping her in the cavernous space and pulling her close.

Her heart pounded against her chest as their eyes met. The hanging garden lights that illuminated the space shone in his eyes. She felt the same heat pass between them as before, his intensity unmistakable this time.

"Alison, anyone who sees you as nothing but a placeholder is blind. You are amazing."

"Are you sure you're not talking to Isobel?" she asked, teasing him with a smile.

Jack shook his head. "It's easier for me to take you into my arms pretending to be Captain Drake than it is being plain Jack Morrison, but costume or no costume, it's you. It's been you."

Alison's breath hitched as Jack drew her closer, his lips, soft and warm, brushing lightly against her own. His warmth spread through her like an early spring, and she laid her hand against his cheek in a silent request for more. Their lips met again, still gentle, but more certain, lingering. When they parted, she gazed into his eyes again to see a tenderness added to the heat that filled her chest.

"I've wanted to do that ever since I saw you clutch your pearls, Alison Hughes. That gasp of yours was too much to bear. When you did it again as I pulled you close for that customer picture, I nearly forgot myself on the spot."

Jack

Jack returned Alison's gaze, so full of warmth and surprise, and couldn't believe he'd told her how he felt.

"It's not just the costume?" she asked, sending shivers down his spine when she laid her hand against the back of his neck.

He allowed himself a shy smile. "I'm not going to lie, Alison. You showing up in that costume last week is the realization of my boyhood dreams. Honestly? If you called me Captain, I'd probably help you move a couch or rob a bank. My favorite thing about it, though, is that I had an excuse to put my arms around you for two straight weeks before summoning the courage to tell you how I feel. Captain Drake had no idea how lucky he was."

Alison smiled at him, for him alone, and Jack realized he couldn't remember the last time he felt that happy. "Now you *will* have to report me to the labor board," she said.

He released her from his arms, still holding her warm hand as they opened the door and stepped into the biting wind to reach the restaurant. "I don't think I have a case. After all, you've never hired me."

They finished dinner in time to reach the theater, where Melissa and Robb had saved seats beside them. Robb, dressed in costume, gave Jack a knowing look as he watched them approach, holding hands. Melissa looked smugger than Jack had known she could.

Jack felt like a teenager, holding hands with Alison during the movie. He marveled at the joy of sharing the most romantic movie he knew with a woman he had feelings for. He also wondered how, at 32, this was the first time it had ever happened.

Walking to the parking lot afterward, Jack and Alison bid goodbye to Melissa and Robb, then stopped at Alison's car door. She shivered against the chilly February evening breeze, and Jack opened his coat to wrap her inside next to him. She obliged, reaching inside his jacket to wrap her arms around him.

"Thank you for a wonderful evening, Jack." The look in her eyes pressed the breath from his lungs.

"It really was wonderful, wasn't it?" Their lips met for another kiss, harder this time than before. Her embrace tightened, fingers pressing into his back as he pulled her closer and she arched into his body, deepening their kiss. It was his turn to gasp this time as currents of desire passed between them.

Don't ruin this.

Lightheaded, he rested his forehead against hers, saying, "I think Mac is probably wondering what happened to me."

"Bella, too," Alison breathed. "I'll talk to you tomorrow, Captain?"

As if I could stay away.

Jack nodded. "Tomorrow." He stood by as Alison climbed into her car, then waited until he started his truck to drive away. On the drive home, Jack thought about how Isobel should have worn glasses.

CHAPTER FIFTEEN

Free Labor

Sunday, February 5

Alison

Alison woke the following morning to a message from Jack.

> **Jack**: Thanks again for a wonderful evening. Hope you have a good week.
> **Alison**: You too. Good luck with your next column. What will that one be?
> **Jack**: Multi-part series on social media lonely hearts scams.
> **Alison**: Good one! Sounds intriguing. I'll send you the info for the final weekend of your forced labor later.
> **Jack**: Please don't put me in wings and a diaper.
> **Alison**: You'll just have to see, won't you?

Despite her banter, Alison realized she would miss having Jack at the store after Valentine's Day. It was too easy to become accustomed to his presence there. Hopefully, after the previous night, she could count on seeing him outside the store.

While she showered, her phone pinged with another message.

> **Brittany**: Quinn left a note for me to give to you when you were alone. I couldn't get you by yourself last night, so I'm just sending it today. Hope it's not too late.
>
> **Alison**: Too late? From Quinn? I doubt it. Was it about my book?
>
> **Brittany**: No, he said that Mindy Penfold's novel was about Jack Morrison. You know, *Bylines and Betrayals*?
>
> **Alison**: MP? Saw an interview saying her book was based on a past romance gone wrong. I didn't know she was Jack's ex. How would Quinn know?
>
> **Brittany**: Beats me. Don't know why he would care either. I'm just passing on the message because he said you have him blocked.
>
> **Alison:** Thanks for letting me know.

Quinn would find a way to ruin things, just to spite me.

Alison pulled up her library app and borrowed an audio copy of Mindy Penfold's book. Happily Ever After Books didn't stock that genre. It was a novel about a woman overcoming a harrowing, psychologically abusive relationship with a cheating louse of a man to become a strong, independent person.

Mindy's interview had struck Alison wrong. Her airy voice and doe eyes had seemed performative. Alison didn't want to victim blame, so she dismissed her feelings and promptly forgot about it.

Was the antagonist really based on Jack Morrison?

Washing and folding her laundry, she kept speeding the narration up as if the faster it went, the faster she could get this over with. Alison did her best to overlook the terrible pacing, inconsistencies, and character development to concentrate on the details and the plot. It was a novel, not a memoir, she reminded herself, as she listened to the description of the Snow White-type heroine and her mustache-twirling villain of a journalist boyfriend.

At first, Alison laughed at the physical description of the boyfriend as a hulking, intimidating bruiser of a man, someone who did not in the least resemble Jack. Then, when she got down to details: verbal tics, habits, and background, Alison could tell that the characterization was based on him. She frowned, listening to the book on her headphones as she walked Bella around the complex.

Still, it's a novel. It's fiction, and not very good fiction. Was there even an editor?

On the way to brunch with Melissa, Alison finished listening to the sensationalized tale. The heroine's discovery of her boyfriend's cheating, so like Alison's discovery of Quinn's infidelity, and her daring escape from the abusive relationship days before their wedding, lined up, in a way, with Jack's accounting of the end of their relationship. Alison didn't know what to believe. Could the man who tucked Bella under his coat in the rain really be the monster in this book?

Even if the character is based on Jack, it's fiction. I'll talk to Melissa.

By the time she joined her friend at the table, Alison, who had begun the day on an emotional high, felt the stress of her confusion taking over.

"What's up?" Melissa asked after seeing Alison's expression. "After watching you two together last night, I thought you would be floating on air today."

After ordering, Alison recounted her morning to Melissa.

"*Bylines and Betrayals?* I know the book has been selling a ton of copies, but I heard it was awful fictional abuse porn."

"It was terrible. I swear half of it was written by AI. It sounded like English, but it didn't quite make sense, which would add up for it to have been written and published so soon after it supposedly happened," Alison said. "But then there are the parts that line up with what Jack told me."

They paused while the server set their plates down.

"You should ask him," Melissa said. "Look, people write revenge novels. It doesn't make them gospel."

"Ask him what? Hey, Jack. My slimy ex told me that this novel was written about you. Are you actually an abusive piece of garbage?" Alison put her napkin on her lap.

Melissa took a bite of her eggs. "I see your point. What will you do?"

"I was hoping you could tell me," Alison said.

"Be careful? Watch how he acts? I mean, Jack was prickly at first, but he was never mean, was he?"

"No. But I couldn't spot a cheater when it was Quinn. What if my radar is broken?" Alison pushed her glasses up before cutting into her French toast.

Jack

That evening, Robb arrived at Jack's apartment, pizza in hand. Mac sat up on his haunches, waiting for Robb either to greet him or to drop the pizza. Jack was never quite sure which. After placing the pizza on the counter, Robb bent down to pet the orange, fluffy monster before removing his coat.

"Look at this. Not only do you have clean clothes and a decent haircut, you've also shoveled out your apartment," Robb said. "Either you have a crush on me, or you're spiffing yourself up to impress Alison."

"You're not my type. Too high maintenance. I already have a cat, remember?"

"I knew you two would get together the minute you referred to her as a 'crazy book lady.' I didn't even have to see what a cute little book nerd she was. You fell for her at first sight."

"Not true at all. It took two weeks," Jack said with a smile. "Then two more before I dared tell her. Which superhero movie are we on?"

"The eighth, I think," Robb said, grabbing a slice of pizza and a can of soda.

Jack pulled out his phone to look up the movie, then served himself a slice, placing an empty pot on top of the pizza box to deter the cat. "Thanks for coming over tonight. I felt so guilty for leaving Mac alone for so long yesterday, I wanted to make up for it. How did your evening with Melissa go?"

"Fantastic. Well, it was for me, at least. I hope it was for her, too. You never know, do you?"

"Sometimes you do," Jack said, dropping onto the couch to hear a dangerous level of strain from the furniture, which predated his student loans.

"Really?" Robb said, raising his eyebrows.

"Nothing like that. We said goodbye at the car. I don't want to rush things. Like her employees say, she's a nice lady."

"So, what are you going to do after next week? Will you keep hanging around the store, giving her puppy dog eyes and free labor? Maybe you'll let her put bows in your hair like she does with Bella."

"You're the one who told me to spend as much time as possible there," Jack said. "For research."

"And look what you discovered." Robb took a huge bite of pizza, trying to keep it from Mac. "Seriously, though, what are you going to do together?"

"I don't know. Book things? Museum stuff? Go out to eat? Maybe I will keep hanging out at the bookstore and giving her free labor. It's worked out so far. She's gotta meet my kid someday." He nodded toward Mac, trying to ignore the scratches the cat had inscribed in the table's glass.

"You might want to wait to bring her over here, Jack," Robb said. "This place is fine for having the guys over, but it's still kind of decorated in 'depressed bachelor' style."

Jack looked around, taking in the ramshackle furniture in his cramped apartment. He thought he'd be farther along in life at his age. "With friends like you," he said with a sigh, starting the movie.

Still, what do I have to offer, except for a profile piece, some shelf-dusting, and a cat who will probably like her more than he likes me?

CHAPTER SIXTEEN
Battle Plans

Wednesday, February 8

Alison

Alison waited with Bella in the parking lot on Wednesday morning. She had decided to disregard Quinn's warning. After all, Quinn was a liar and a cheater, and Alison had no reason to trust him. Still, she had heard little from Jack since their text on Sunday, aside from an acknowledgment of receiving the information for that week's theme and event.

It was an unseasonably warm February morning, and Alison had left her coat at home in favor of a soft pink cardigan. She had smiled when she fastened her pearls, recalling what Jack had said on Saturday night.

When Jack's truck pulled up beside her car, Alison got out and opened the car door to let Bella greet him. The little dog, sporting a pink bow, launched herself at him, her front paws reaching the knees of his uncharacteristically tidy chinos. He picked Bella up, greeting her, but treated Alison as if Saturday had never happened. Her stomach sank. Had he regretted it already?

"Thanks for getting all that information out to the events lists. With all the food vendors participating in our Better Than Sex dessert event, it would be a shame if nobody showed." Alison pulled the wagon from the back of the car and snapped it open before dropping her bags into it.

"So, 20% off all food-themed romances? I wasn't aware that was a thing," he said.

"You should know by now that there's romance for every theme imaginable," Alison said, the wagon rattling as she pulled it across the parking lot. "Are you a dessert guy?"

"Sometimes," he said. "I guess it depends on my mood. Did you get many online orders for this week?"

"A fair number. Not as many as last week, but last week was phenomenal," she said, giving him a knowing smile.

"It was, wasn't it?" he agreed, seeming to let his guard down as they boarded the elevator together. Bella wriggled impatiently in his arms when the door opened, and Jack set her down, holding her leash as the three of them walked down the hallway. As they neared the store, Jack's head snapped to face something in his periphery as a flash of fur disappeared into a corner. "*What* was that?"

"Mill cat," Alison answered, unlocking the store's door. "They're feral cats that live here to keep the rodents away. They do a great job, too. Bella had a run-in with one, once, and learned that not all friend-shaped things are friends."

"Doesn't anyone take care of them?" Jack asked.

Alison chuckled. "Of course, they do. The cats get food, beds, litter boxes, regular vet care, and all that. It comes out of our rent, like we would pay any other pest control. And they're fixed, so no kittens. Guaranteed housing, food security, health insurance and housekeeping. These cats live better than most people I know."

"Oh. That makes me feel better," Jack said, releasing Bella for her celebratory lap around the store. "People aren't always as nice to cats as they are to dogs."

Jack's concern for the mill cats warmed Alison's heart, making her feel better about her decision to ignore Quinn's warning. "You're not as prickly as you like to pretend, Jack. Between you and me, there are days I think those cats have the right idea, avoiding humans as much as possible while staying on the payroll."

"You? Aren't you an extrovert?"

"I'd say I'm down the middle of the road. I get peopled-out, too. You, on the other hand…"

He huffed in acknowledgment. "Introvert all the way. Robb is the one who drags me out of the house, otherwise it would just be Mac and me most of the time. The time I've spent here is the most socializing I've done in ages. Robb says it's done me good to get aired out a little."

Alison took her purse and laptop from the wagon, then pulled it aside to fill it with packaged orders later. "Speaking of Mac, I have a question. How did you end up with a big, fancy purebred cat? I took you more for the type who would go to the Humane Society or the shelter, or adopted a cat who turned up on his doorstep."

"You would be right. My ex wanted a big, fancy purebred cat. I was resistant to the idea of any pets, considering our schedules at the time. When she left, she didn't want Mac any longer, so I let her go and kept the cat. If you ask me, I got the better end of the deal."

"She didn't *want* him?" Alison was aghast. There was another strike against Mindy.

"I guess he didn't fit in with her new life. I'm pretty sure he likes me better, anyway." He raised an eyebrow at her. "Not that I blame him."

"Quinn would have taken Bella over my dead body."

"Bella's not what he wants from you, is she?" Jack asked, concern in his voice.

"He wouldn't dare." Alison frowned, then sighed. "He wants the book."

Jack paused for a moment as the light of realization entered his eyes. "*That* book?"

"Yes, the copy of *Pride and Prejudice* that belonged to his grandmother." She released a puff of air.

Jack shook his head. "Oof. Leave it to me to create a disaster with a cup of coffee."

"I hadn't decided whether to give it to him. Quinn gave the book to me as a gift long before we broke up, and it's rightfully mine. I would only have surrendered it so I'd never have to see him again, but Huntsville's both a big town and a small one. Giving up the book would have been no guarantee."

"I hope I've been a little help in making up for what I've cost you, even though I'm not your most valuable employee."

She felt a flicker of guilt for dumping the whole *Pride and Prejudice* disaster on him, but he'd been dying to know the truth, and she was tired of letting his imagination run wild.

"You may not be the most experienced bookstore employee," she said, stepping close enough to touch the warm sleeve of his sweater, "but you have other fine qualities." She rose on her toes and gave him a quick kiss, light as a punctuation mark. "Seriously, you've done a bang-up job with the promo notices, and you've made the in-store events more fun than they've ever been. I appreciate everything you've done for the store. And for me."

She smoothed the collar peeking from his sweater before she stepped back, trying and failing to hide the little smile tugging at her mouth.

Jack

As Jack dragged the sandwich board into the hallway and unlocked the door, Alison dropped Bella behind the baby gate. She turned on the register while Jack set up displays of the books she had pulled for her promotion earlier in the week. The crisp new paperbacks filled his nose with their woody smell as he arranged them on the tables. He placed the sales signs among them so they wouldn't fall with the first brush of a customer's purse.

She kissed me this morning. She didn't seem to have regrets about Saturday, but what does she see in me? When I'm not in a costume, I'm just a sad bachelor. Why would she still want to be with me once she learns what I'm like outside of the store?

He stole glances at Alison as she wrinkled her brow at the register display, a pensive Sexy Librarian in a frilly apron, then looked away before she could catch him. After she finished helping him set up the displays, Alison excused herself to pack orders in the back, and Jack watered the plants trailing around the tops of the bookcases.

"Jack?" she said as he poured the remaining water into Bella's dish. "Do you want to go over the plans for Saturday's event before customers start arriving today?"

"Sure. How will it work?"

Alison pulled her planning sheet to the side as she stood at the worktable, an invitation for Jack to stand beside her. "We're setting up in the hallway, again, only this time it's an open event, sort of like when they used to set the artist markets up inside. Each vendor will be responsible for their own sales, but we'll be maintaining the little tall tables set up in the middle. Unfortunately, that means we'll be doing some bussing, since people can't be counted on to clean up after themselves. Is that okay with you?" She seemed hesitant.

"Of course it is. I did restaurant work in college."

Alison's face relaxed at his answer. "Okay, I didn't want you to think I was taking advantage of you."

"If it's not beneath you, why would it be beneath me?" Jack put his hand on her waist, something that was so easy the weekend before, but seemed so much more difficult when he was just Jack.

She met his eyes, mumbling, "I don't know. I felt like I had to ask."

After covering the rest of the plans, Alison posted them on the whiteboard above her desk. "So, battle plans in place? I'm not used to wrangling this many different people. At least Melissa and Monique will be there to help, although I haven't heard from Brittany yet."

"You're planning on this being a big deal, aren't you?" he asked.

"It's dessert, and right before Valentine's Day. I don't know how it will effect store sales, but I'm expecting a good deal of traffic."

"What about Valentine's Day themed books?" Jack asked, his brow wrinkled.

Alison blinked at him, then seemed to panic. "Of course! I was so wrapped up in my other promotions, I forgot. I should have had them out for weeks!"

"Hey," he said, "there's always room for another display. I'll bet you've more than made up for Valentine's Day themed book sales in other promotional sales."

"I don't even have any holiday signage up."

"It's not like people don't know, Alison. Take a breath. I didn't mean to upset you. We'll fix it."

Alison touched her string of pearls, focusing somewhere far away. Jack felt guilt spike in his ribs. This wasn't about displays. Something in her had snapped sideways.

He tipped his head into her line of vision, softer this time. "We've got it, Alison. I'll condense the displays, you pull the books. It's fixable."

She nodded, but her eyes were still somewhere else entirely.

Something's wrong. Something she won't tell me. God, did she wake up regretting everything?

Jack made space for the new displays while Alison pulled books for them, stacking them on the cart.

"Alison, are you okay?" he asked. "I know you like to be on top of things, but this doesn't seem to be the kind of reaction you normally have to something we can fix."

"Are you telling me that I'm overreacting?" Her voice was sharp with suspicion.

"No, I'm asking whether there's something bothering you in addition to this." Jack began assembling the displays.

"No, yes, I mean, there shouldn't be, but I don't know what to think."

Oh, she does regret it.

"What is it?" he asked.

"I don't feel like I can talk about it right now," she said. "Let's just fix this mess. Thanks for bringing it to my attention."

Jack finished the first display as Alison worked on the second. "If you feel like you want to talk later, I'm happy to listen."

"Yeah, thanks," she said.

CHAPTER SEVENTEEN
Team Lift

Saturday, February 11

Alison

Alison rested her hands on the steering wheel, waiting in the rainy parking lot for Jack to show up Saturday morning, almost hoping that he wouldn't. Thursday and Friday had been as awkward as Wednesday had been, with Jack acting defensive about everything from dusting to customer interactions, leaving Alison unsure how to respond.

She thought she had disregarded Quinn's warning to decide for herself, but doubt remained with Jack's unpredictable behavior. He would compliment her outfit and offer to load the car, then leave her standing alone in the parking lot like a stranger.

Her concern would have to wait for another day, she determined. With the Better Than Sex dessert event that evening, Alison was too busy to worry about her romantic situation, whatever that was.

Bella, tired of sitting in the car, climbed between the front seats to sit on Alison's lap.

"Really, Baby Bella?" Alison asked, lifting the dog off herself and placing her in the passenger seat. "Your feet are still wet."

As she began typing a text to Jack to ask whether he still intended to work, his truck pulled up next to her car. Pulling her jacket hood up, Alison climbed out, Bella under her arm. Jack approached the car in his own raincoat and took Bella from her. She loaded the wagon with all the props and supplies she had brought from home, covering it with a plastic bag to protect the contents on the way in.

"You ready?" she asked, trying to shake the weather's gloom as they made their way to the elevator.

"I guess," Jack said, his enthusiasm as damp as the weather.

Alison hated to admit it, but she felt the same. The difference was that this was her event, so she had to feign enthusiasm.

Fake it 'til you make it, girl.

Once they entered the elevator, she took in the sight of Jack holding her wet dog and smiled. "We three are something special this morning," she said. "I hope the rain doesn't ruin the event tonight."

"Yeah." Jack set Bella down with a plop. She shook off the rain, flinging her damp bow at Alison's feet. Alison sighed as she picked the ribbon up and stuffed it into her pocket.

"Good thing you're not the main attraction, Baby Bella. You're a mess."

They trudged to the store, and Jack followed her to the

office, where he removed his raincoat to expose a faded t-shirt and some old jeans. He looked like he had slept in his clothes. Alison tried to ignore his clothing choice, but it felt so *personal*.

"Shall we set up all our tables?" Alison led Jack to the storage room near the end of the hallway. "Pick your poison," she said, gesturing at the carts holding tables and chairs.

Jack grabbed one and pushed it toward the door, not slowing down when Alison tried to warn him he was in danger of crashing into the doorway. She flinched when he hit it, pressing her lips together and helping him back the cart away from the door to steer it through. Once he was through, Alison pushed the other cart after him.

"Let's team lift the tables," Alison said.

"I've got it." Jack reached in and almost instantly smashed his hand.

"I offered to do a team lift," Alison said, trying not to wince at the bright-red skin. "Those tables are awful to do on your own."

"You manage," Jack shot back, too fast, too sharp.

"I smash my hands every time, like you just did. I was trying to save you the pain. Are you ready to team lift now?"

He muttered something low and miserable.

"Pardon?"

"Yes." His shoulders fell, the fight draining out of him all at once, and Alison felt her irritation twist into something darker…closer to dread.

What is wrong with this man?

Jack

Jack winced, trying to ignore the throbbing, insistent pulse in his hand as Alison helped him lift tables from the cart. Her clipped responses and skittish lack of eye contact made him feel like she was pulling away. Maybe she'd hoped whatever spark had flared between them would die once the pirate costumes went back in storage. He'd woken with a dull ache in his chest that morning and asked himself what the point of trying even was. He would fulfill his promise, do the grunt work for the event, finish the store's business profile, and then get out of Alison's way.

The banging and clatter of setup assaulted his ears as they arranged tables to her precise specifications. Jack unfolded the metal vendor chairs with a hollow clang while Alison smoothed heavy black tablecloths and set glass candle globes in perfect rows. She didn't touch him once, didn't joke, didn't look at him long enough for warmth to build. Jack kept his distance, afraid of embarrassing them both with misplaced affection.

They finished setting up just in time to open the store. Alison rushed to start the register, asking Jack to place reserved signs on the tables before customers began cluttering them.

She took a deep breath. "Last storefront business day before Valentine's Day. Glad this will be over."

Then you'll be rid of me.

She disappeared into customer interactions. Jack kept busy tidying the shelves and ushering people away from the reserved tables until Brittany arrived, crisp in black slacks and a red button-down.

"What happened to you?" she asked, eyeing him like he'd crawled out of a drain. "You look like someone dragged you here from rotting in front of the TV."

"Thanks for that," he said.

"You're aware this is Alison's biggest event, and you showed up like you just finished mowing the lawn? Rude. I wondered how much of Penfold's book was true."

Jack's stomach dropped. "None of it is true, okay? That's why it's a novel. Does Alison know Mindy's my ex?"

"Last Saturday, Quinn told me to warn her before she got hurt," Brittany said. "I emailed her Sunday."

"Well, that explains a lot," he said. "She never even asked me about it. Why should I bother trying?"

"It doesn't look like you did try." Brittany folded her arms. "She knows better than to believe everything she reads, but you showed up today proving her wrong. That's too bad, because she really liked you."

"She...did?" Jack asked. "How would you know?"

"Everyone knew." Brittany rolled her eyes. "But if you're going to act like this event doesn't matter to her on your last day here, I guess you saved her some heartache. You still owe her a stellar business profile, or else."

Her disgusted look pierced straight through him. His faded T-shirt didn't say he'd messed up; it said he didn't care at all.

He retreated into the hallway to call Robb.

"Hey, Jack," Robb answered. "Aren't you supposed to be at the store?"

"I *am* at the store, but I need a change of clothes. I screwed up," Jack said.

"Did you spill something again?"

Jack dragged a hand across his face. "No. Can you help me out? You have my apartment code."

"I don't have a key to your gate, Jack. You'll have to get them yourself."

"I can't. The vendors are arriving any minute. Can I borrow something of yours?"

"My pants are too long, but I'll bring you one of my shirts when Melissa and I head over."

"Thanks," Jack said. "I owe you."

"See you soon."

He shoved his phone into his pocket just as the first vendor rounded the corner.

CHAPTER EIGHTEEN
Kick Rocks

Saturday, February 11

Alison

Reaching into her desk drawer, Alison pulled out her emergency antiperspirant. The baby-powder scent calmed her a little as she awkwardly reached through her collar for an extra swipe.

"You know it's a day when you have to pull out the desk deodorant," Monique said, stepping over the baby gate and bending to pet Bella. "Are these catering aprons for us?"

Alison exhaled with relief. "I'm so glad you're here. I keep going back and forth. If we wear them, will it look like the store's unstaffed?"

Monique tilted her head. "True. But it'd be nice to cover up Jack's ratty outfit. Man looks like he doesn't work *anywhere.*"

Alison rolled her eyes. "Did you notice he was off yesterday too? He's been like this all week. We were getting along so well."

That earned her a side-eye. "You've been off, too."

"What do you do when you don't know where you stand?" Alison asked. "I've been tiptoeing around him since Wednesday. The last thing I need today is another thing to stress about."

"Then here's the plan," Monique said. "You two have got to talk after tonight. Not before. For today, I'll handle Jack and the customers. Brittany runs the register. You play hostess. Will Melissa will show up? Actually, of course she will, I don't need to ask. She and Jack can take tables in the aprons. How's that?"

The tension leaked from Alison's shoulders. "Perfect. Thank you for being my brain."

"You've done great," Monique said, "but you overdid it this year. It's too much stress for one woman."

"I know." Alison sighed. "Things have been a lot, especially with Quinn pestering me. Remind me you're first in line for a raise."

"Depends. When was *your* last raise?"

Alison winced. "We do not need to talk about that."

"Then I'm second. I'll settle for an increased employee discount."

"That can be arranged. We'll call it the Assistant Manager's Discount."

Monique spotted Melissa. "There she is." She grabbed the aprons and strode to the front.

Alison took a last sip from her giant tumbler, kissed Bella goodbye, and headed out to join the others. Melissa spotted her immediately.

"Hiding already?" Melissa teased, already wearing an apron.

"Preparing to hit the stage," Alison said, hugging her.

Melissa grabbed another apron. "For Robb. He insisted on helping."

"That's sweet."

"He's still trying to impress me," Melissa said with a wink. "Might as well put him to work. He also brought a shirt for Jack."

"Really?" Alison narrowed her eyes. "How did he know?"

"Jack called him in a panic," Melissa said. "Said he screwed up. Is he okay? Are you okay?"

"Me personally? Too much on my plate. I'll celebrate when Valentine's Day is over."

"Well, that answers the you-as-in-you-two part of my question."

"I don't know what's going on with him," Alison said. "And I don't have time today."

"Coffee tomorrow," Melissa said. "You both need clarity."

"Monique said the same thing."

"Then listen to Monique," Melissa said. "Ready?"

"It's showtime." Alison scratched Bella for luck and followed her out.

When she reached the front, Jack was tying an apron on over a fresh shirt—one a little too big, but worlds better than the sagging T-shirt. He gave her a polite, distant smile. It made her stomach twist.

Oh well.

Alison greeted the vendors, bought one item from each, and stashed her bag in the back. Brittany flashed a thumbs up as Alison returned.

She grabbed an extra fork, banged it against the metal frame, and called, "Welcome, y'all, to the Better Than Sex Dessert Event at Happily Ever After Books…"

The crowd applauded. Alison circulated, smiling, chatting, counting down the minutes until it ended. About an hour in, she saw the last person she wanted: Quinn. And beside him—Mindy Penfold. The red mermaid hair was unmistakable. Alison wondered if the breathy voice she'd heard in interviews was real or just branding.

And I thought he was out of surprises.

"Alison," Quinn said, projecting so half the hallway turned. "Last event before the holiday? I thought I'd bring my fiancée, Mindy Penfold, best-selling author."

"Hi," Mindy breathed, offering a limp handshake.

Alison dropped it quickly. "Pleased to meet you."

"You two have something in common," Quinn said. "Alison tried to write a book once."

"That's sweet," Mindy cooed. "So did my ex. What a coincidence. There he is now. Jaaack!"

Jack looked up from wiping a table, and with visible effort, walked over.

"Here to enjoy dessert?" Alison asked stiffly.

"That, and checking whether you carry my book," Quinn said smugly. "We're on our way to a show."

Mindy giggled. "Quinn said you might be here, Jack. He told me you're working retail to make ends meet, and now you're bussing tables. It's too bad—not everyone can be a successful author, I guess."

Jack's face flushed scarlet, jaw clenching. "I'm helping a friend."

He's helping a friend. Now I see where I stand.

"I am not bussing tables to make ends meet," he bit out. "And I am not working *retail*."

He spat the last word so viciously that Alison felt it like a slap.

Mindy feigned fear, hiding behind Quinn. The man moved between Quinn and Mindy as if he were protecting the woman from a snarling beast, but Alison could see the satisfaction gleaming in his eyes.

That was the final crack.

"You want my book, Quinn?" Alison snapped. "Fine. I'll give you my book."

She stormed to the back, snatched the damaged *Pride and Prejudice,* and shoved it into his hands. "There. Consider it a wedding gift. I hope you don't cheat on her like you did on me."

Quinn looked at the ruined copy. "What happened to it?"

"Ask him." Alison pointed at Jack. "I have nothing left to say to any of you. Apparently I'm a joke, so no more pretending. I'm done."

Every eye in the hall tracked her as she bolted to her office. She hooked up Bella, grabbed her purse and the desserts, and shoved the shop keys into Monique's hand.

"Please close up tonight."

She passed the trio again, stopping only long enough to say, "Mindy, honey, here's a tip: you're not an author if the computer does the writing." Then she strode off, trying to escape before she began to cry. Melissa hurried beside her, promising she and Monique would handle the rest and bring Alison's things by later.

Jack tried to follow, but Melissa turned back. "I think you've said enough, Morrison. You're fired."

Alison reached her car in the rain, coat forgotten. She loaded Bella, tossed everything in the passenger seat, and drove home blasting a Taylor Swift breakup mix just below Bella's pain threshold.

When she pulled up at her cottage, her heart sank. Someone had emptied her Little Free Library, every book gone.

"Figures, Bella. Try to make the world better, and someone ruins it."

She dumped her things inside, grabbed an umbrella, and took Bella into the rain.

"At least I have Melissa, Monique, and Brittany," she told the dog. "And you. None of you think I'm a joke. The rest of them can kick rocks, Baby Bella."

The dog did her business quickly and tugged to go back inside.

"Good girl," Alison murmured. "Let's put on pajamas and watch *Legally Blonde*."

Jack

The moment the words left Jack's mouth, he wanted to punch himself in the face.

With one well-aimed jab, Mindy had slipped under his skin again, poking every bruise she'd left behind. Jack felt dread coil in his gut as Quinn smirked, waiting for Alison to fetch the ruined book, while Mindy hid behind him like a helpless ingénue for the benefit of her audience. They were both using him to sell more copies of her trash novel, and he'd practically gift-wrapped the performance for them.

Quinn and Mindy were selfish, cruel cheats who deserved each other. But what Jack said—*that* careless, arrogant line—had wounded Alison far more than anything either of them had done on purpose. Her store was her life. And he'd stood there, in front of God and half of Huntsville, and acted like it was beneath him.

A knife didn't hold a candle to that kind of damage.

It wasn't even *true*. Not that it mattered.

Melissa had done the right thing, stopping him before he could chase Alison with a pathetic apology. Nothing he said in that moment would have softened the blow. He stripped off the apron, handing it to Robb with a defeated slump. "Grab my raincoat before you two close up?" he muttered.

Then he retreated into the stairwell. His footsteps echoed off the white concrete. The humid, faintly bat-guano-scented air tightened his throat. At the bottom, he shoved open the heavy exterior door. Rain poured off the roof in sheets, lit by the pale security lights. The cold pierced straight through Robb's oversized shirt, but Jack barely felt it.

Alison's parking space beside his truck was empty.
We always left together.

He dug out his phone, thumb hovering over her name. There was nothing he could type that wouldn't make everything worse. He tossed the phone onto the passenger seat and drove home in silence.

Mac tried to trip him the second he stepped inside, twining around his legs and yowling for dinner. Jack bent, stroking the cat's thick fur.

"Buddy, I don't deserve you."

One glimpse of himself in the bathroom mirror—soaked, pathetic, shell-shocked—and he understood why Alison had walked away. It was her biggest event of the year, and he'd shown up in a shirt that looked like it had lost a fight with a weed whacker. Even if things had been over before he'd arrived, she deserved better.

He changed into sweatpants, dug the remote out of the couch cushions, brushed crumbs off it, and put on *Plundering Seas*. The familiarity hurt, but he let it.

When the credits rolled, Robb called from the gate. Jack buzzed him in and waited. Mac galloped to greet him when he entered with pizza and a bag containing Jack's jacket and the cursed T-shirt.

"Mindy did it again," Robb announced, setting the pizza down. "But this time you did half the work for her. When will you learn?" He paused, eyeing the TV. "And you're watching *Plundering Seas*? You punishing yourself?"

"Yes," Jack said. "Why shouldn't I? I even managed to ruin your night with Melissa. She won't dump you because of me, will she?"

"Don't flatter yourself," Robb said. "She's furious at you, but she's not redirecting it at me. Neither of them is."

"How did the rest of the event go?"

"You ended it. That was some top-tier spectacle you four cooked up."

Jack groaned. "Brittany is going to put a hit out on me. She already threatened to cancel me."

"I talked her down," Robb said. "And I think Monique won't actually track you through the woods. But the real problem? Alison didn't believe Mindy's book was about you—until you acted exactly like the guy in it today."

"So she thinks I'm an abusive jerk now?" Jack asked.

"I don't know what she thinks," Robb said, pulling two slices from the box, "but she didn't care what *they* said. She cared what *you* said."

Jack sank onto the couch. The old thing squeaked, then snapped, sending the cushion sinking nearly to the floor.

"Great," he muttered, climbing out.

Robb took the other cushion, leaving his friend with the other arm of the sectional. "Jack, she cares about you."

Jack shoved Mac away from his plate. "I stomped on her heart in front of everyone. When she left, she lumped me in with Quinn and Mindy. And she was right."

Robb's expression softened. "I'm afraid so."

Jack stared down at the slice in his hands. "I finally found an amazing woman who gave me a chance, and I blew it. I don't want to lose her. What should I do?"

Robb took a thoughtful sip of soda. "I don't know, man, but it's up to you to make it right."

Alison

By the time the closing credits rolled on *Legally Blonde*, Alison had eaten three desserts and still didn't feel better. Bella bounded off the couch at the sound of the doorbell, nails clicking on the wood floor.

"I brought Chinese," Melissa announced, handing Alison the warm paper bag. "Where do you want your laptop?"

"Wherever." Alison set the bag on the table, grabbed plates, and tried not to feel like a deflated balloon. "Are you here to help me plan revenge?"

"More like emotional triage." Melissa kicked off her shoes, dropped the laptop in the office, and rejoined her at the table. She unpacked containers of stir-fry, filling the small cottage with comforting, greasy aromas.

"Thank you for everything today. There was no way I could stay. That was humiliating." Alison spooned General Tso's and rice onto her plate. "I have no words for how demeaning it was when Jack said what he did."

"I guarantee that you were the only one who came out of that circus looking better." Melissa dug into her beef and broccoli. "I knew we were doomed the second Quinn strutted in with Mindy Penfold. Did you know they're engaged?"

"No idea. And Jack didn't either. Quinn only met him last week." Alison snapped her chopsticks apart and waved Bella away from her plate.

"Well, Jack looked blindsided." Melissa pointed a warning chopstick at Bella, who was begging for beef. "I'm not allowed allowed to share, Bella. Your mom is heartless," she informed the dog.

"Bella has her own treats. And yes, I was surprised, but not enough to show it."

Melissa smirked. "Resignation and boredom are sisters. Same family. Neither is shock."

"I hope Quinn was disappointed." Alison's voice brightened just a hair. "He definitely didn't like getting his grandmother's book back the way it was."

"He wanted that exact copy. You delivered." Melissa grinned around a giant hunk of broccoli.

"That Penfold woman..." Alison wrinkled her nose. "I don't buy that she looked or sounded like that when she and Jack were together. The baby-voice, the limp hand, the whole porcelain-doll persona...it's a bit much."

"That AI comment you threw out? She looked like she wanted to yank your hair out."

"I wish she had. Then I could've yanked hers. We'd see how well those extensions were attached." Alison snorted. "People forget how strong you get hauling boxes of books all day."

"I'd have jumped in." Melissa nodded solemnly. "Girl fight. Glorious."

Silence fell for a beat before Alison whispered, "Do you think Jack meant what he said? The way he said *retail* made it sound so…dirty."

"I doubt he meant it the way it came out, but he owes you a massive apology. For the comment, the attitude, the meltdown—the whole thing. You both have past relationship trauma to untangle, but only one of you detonated it in public today."

"How much mess is left for me to deal with tomorrow?"

Melissa lifted an eyebrow. "Did you really think we'd leave you with that? Monique and I cleaned the place within an inch of its life. There's no evidence any crimes occurred."

Tears pricked Alison's eyes. "Will you marry me? My life would be so much easier."

Melissa hugged her tightly. "You don't need to marry me to keep me around. I'm not going anywhere."

CHAPTER NINETEEN

Donuts

Sunday, February 12

Jack

Jack woke to the smell of something warm and awful inches from his face. He blinked blearily into an enormous orange cat butt.

"Mac, why?" he moaned, recoiling. Mac responded with a pleased chirp, purring like a small engine and swishing his tail directly across Jack's nose. "Fine." Jack shoved back the covers and staggered toward the bathroom.

Robb, sensing that Jack's emotional bandwidth was below sea level, had invited him to do laundry at his place. Anything was better than being trapped in a laundromat, marinating in fluorescent light while someone else's playlist rattled the dryers.

With a groan, Jack collected the smelly clothes scattered around his apartment. On impulse, he stripped the bed too, grabbed the towels, and shoved the whole pathetic pile into a basket. Laundry, laptop, keys. He stopped for breakfast burritos on the way out, the warm, savory smell filling the truck and making his stomach lurch with something like hope. Or nausea.

Robb's new complex gleamed in the bright morning light with red brick, a spotless parking lot, and not a hint of mildew. Jack tucked the food safely away from his foul socks and let himself in when the door buzzed. The lobby smelled of free coffee and clean carpets. He took the elevator up to the third floor.

Robb was waiting at the door in the soft morning light. "You sleep okay?" His eyes caught the shadows under Jack's.

"Not really," Jack admitted. He handed off the food and lugged the basket toward the washer. "Let me start this before we eat. I don't want to hijack your whole Sunday."

He tried cramming everything into one overstuffed load before Robb intercepted him. "My appliances aren't built for self-destruction; sort your loads. It's not coin-op here." He nudged the burrito bag. "Come on, before breakfast becomes a disappointment."

They ate at the counter. Jack doused his burrito in hot sauce and confessed he'd brought his laptop because he hadn't started Alison's business profile.

"Did you at least do the interview?" Robb asked.

"No, I kept waiting for the right moment. Then yesterday happened." Jack scrubbed a hand through his hair. "Now it feels impossible."

"You'll have to go with what you already know." Robb sipped his coffee. "And you know a lot."

"When do I even try to talk to her?"

Robb inhaled sharply through his teeth. "Maybe text her.

Ask if she wants to talk. But don't expect anything right away. Yesterday wasn't just bad: it was end-of-the-world bad."

"You mean *I* was end-of-the-world bad," Jack said.

Robb chewed slowly, thinking. "Alison was stressed all week. Melissa said she looked ready to either cry or stab something. But here's the thing: she doesn't hate you." He pointed his fork. "That parting shot she threw at Mindy? That was *for you*. She didn't flinch when Quinn and Mindy insulted her. But the second they went after you, she went nuclear."

Jack blinked. "You think that was about me?"

"Obviously it was about you. Mindy poked your insecurities and you exploded. But that explosion? It probably kept both of them from being carried out on stretchers. Alison looked like she'd have happily gone to jail swinging."

Jack let out a breath he hadn't realized he'd been holding. "I still hope I can get her forgiveness," he said quietly.

"You better," Robb replied. "And whatever you do next has to be very, very good."

Alison

Alison woke to the sound of her doorbell. "Coming," she called as she shuffled through the living room and ordered Bella back before opening the door.

Melissa stood there with a box of Bigfoot's Little Donuts in one hand and a coffee carrier in the other.

"You don't even eat donuts," Alison said, pretending she didn't have a headache and her eyes weren't still puffy from crying herself to sleep after Melissa left the night before.

"I make an exception for Bigfoot once in a while," Melissa said as she kicked off her shoes. "Besides, they're practically in your neighborhood. Let's eat these before they get cold."

"I'd ask what you're doing here, but you brought donuts." Alison's phone chimed. She retrieved it from the bedroom while Melissa set breakfast on the table.

"I'm making sure you got out of bed after turning down my brunch invitation," Melissa said. "Important?" she added when she saw Alison checking her screen.

"Jack. Asking if we can talk."

"You should." Melissa grabbed a coffee and opened the donut box, filling the cottage with the scent of warm cinnamon.

"And I will," Alison said, "but not right now." She sat, took a breath, and let the heat from the box warm her hands. "You're here, and I'm not ready. I told him now isn't a good time."

"That's nice and vague." Melissa used a tiny fork to spear a steaming donut coated in honey and cinnamon sugar. "Mm. Perfect."

"Should I have said I'm waiting until I'm sure I won't cry?" Alison asked. She bit into a donut, blowing the excess heat away as the sweetness and spice burst across her tongue. They were almost juicy.

Donuts should not taste this good.

"I can talk to you about it, but thinking about him trying to apologize or end things or whatever this morning makes my throat close up."

Melissa paused mid-reach, watching her with that irritating gentleness she only used when Alison was about to crack.

"Robb told me Mindy's book was entirely fabricated," Melissa said. "She was the one who cheated on Jack."

Alison's jaw tightened before she answered. "I figured as much. Mindy's a phony. She and Quinn were probably circling each other long before she left Jack." She brushed sugar from her fingers. "But that's not my problem."

"I know. Brittany and Monique said Jack was acting off."

"He was distant all week," Alison said, settling into her chair as if bracing for impact. "And we bickered over unloading tables yesterday. Tables. It felt like he was gearing up to say goodbye, like he'd spent the whole weekend rethinking us and didn't know how to break it to me."

Melissa raised a brow. "Robb says Jack wants to make up."

Alison's eyes flicked up to meet Melissa's. "I do, too," she admitted quietly. "But I have to ask myself whether I want to be with someone who thinks so little of me." She stared into her coffee. "Quinn was always embarrassed by me. Jack basically told me my shop was stupid the day we met. He seemed to come around…until he was cornered yesterday. How do I know he won't say whatever I want to hear right up until the next time he feels embarrassed by me?"

The bitter coffee sharpened the sweetness of the donuts on her tongue.

Melissa shrugged, the motion soft, not dismissive. "You'll have to listen and decide for yourself. Robb knows him, but he's not a psychic, and I lost my crystal ball years ago."

Alison's phone chimed again.

CHAPTER TWENTY
The Rewrite

Tuesday, February 14

Alison

To avoid thinking about Jack, Alison stuffed her Valentine's Day with the most aggressively mundane task she could find: packing online orders at the store. She wrapped each blind date book with almost surgical precision, folding the paper neatly, tucking in stickers, a bookmark, a handwritten thank-you, and a tea bag. The air smelled of paper and bergamot, which unfortunately reminded her of their conversation.

He never did come around to thinking this was worthwhile.

She scooped handfuls of fluffy pink shredded paper into a shipping box, making sure everything inside was cushioned and perfect.

Maybe he's never felt special before.

Bella pawed at her leg until Alison sighed and lifted her up. "Baby Bella, what am I going to do with you?" The dog blinked at her with those ridiculous button eyes. Alison gave her a quick cuddle, then set her down and took a long drink from her tumbler.

Her phone pinged. The newest *Love Is a Scam* column had been posted. Her store profile still hadn't shown up, which irritated her more than she wanted to admit. She hesitated, thumb hovering, debating whether to read it.

Another ping. A text.

Jack.

She took a breath before she opened it.

Jack: *Please don't stop hate-reading me today.*

Her stomach dropped.

Fine. I'll read his Romance Bookstores Are a Scam column.

LOVE IS A SCAM

By Jack Morrison

Love is a scam…except when it isn't.

Sometimes it starts by accident, triggered by something as ridiculous as a spilled cup of coffee and an unpaid debt. Love can be uncomfortable, like wearing rented shoes and an outfit that attracts far more attention than you intended. Love can demand more courage than we think we have, especially when the people closest to us are involved. But love can also be a dream: dizzying, joyful, freeing.

If we're lucky, most of us get to fall in love a few precious times in our lives. But there is a store in Huntsville's Lowe Mill where you can fall in love over and over again and reliably get a happy ending.

Happily Ever After Books, a romance bookstore with pink walls and a bow-wearing little dog, understands love better than any column I've ever written. Here, the staff helps you find the kind of story you're craving, and they do it with genuine care.

The store's proprietor, Alison Hughes, has dedicated her life to happy endings. She knows every length of romance, from novelette to epic, and can find you a theme for anything from bakeries to pirate ships. Her brick-and-mortar shop thrives alongside a flourishing online business, where every order receives a heartfelt thank-you and a beautifully wrapped surprise. Her blind date books and themed gift boxes are so thoughtfully crafted that I've heard rumors Santa Claus is requesting tutorials.

Alison, with her bright optimism and unrelenting enthusiasm, also hosts events that run with the precision of a NASA launch. Her customers return again and again, drawn not just by the books but by the feeling she curates. Even I haven't been immune.

In her pretty pink world, I found myself believing in love again—and, more surprisingly, falling for Alison Hughes.

As a writer, the written word is safer for me. The delete key is merciful; spoken words are not. Sometimes we say things we don't mean and hurt people who deserve better. If we're lucky, we get a chance to apologize.

Alison Hughes, you created something remarkable. You *are* remarkable. I beg you to forgive me for ever making you think I believed anything less, and I hope you'll let me return to your world of Happily Ever Afters.

Alison grabbed a tissue, wiping her eyes as her phone pinged again.

Jack: *Please let me in?*

She peered into the dim hallway outside the store. Jack stood there, dressed in full Captain Drake regalia, holding a package as a peace offering.

Her breath caught.

When she opened the door, he set the package down and pulled her into his arms. His warmth grounded her, but it also made her lightheaded in a way she hadn't felt since their first kiss.

He cares. I'm not an embarrassment or a failure to him.

"I'm sorry, Alison," he whispered. "Will you please forgive me?"

When they kissed, it wasn't fireworks. It was warmth, ache, and apology all braided together. His mouth moved gently against hers, like he was terrified she might pull away but hoping desperately she wouldn't.

She didn't. She leaned in, curling her fingers into the lapel of his ridiculous pirate coat. Her lips parted. It wasn't about the apology anymore. It was about choosing him, choosing to try.

When they finally parted, foreheads resting together, both of them smiling, she felt the shift—the beginning of something worth the risk.

Their lips met again, softer this time, then with a little joyful pressure. Alison buried her hands in his curls, letting herself fall into him for a moment she'd needed far more than she'd admitted.

When they drew apart, she grinned. "Of course I forgive you, Jack. I missed you, and it's only been since Saturday. I could be in trouble here."

Jack gave her a rakish Captain Drake smile. "You are trouble, lass. Glorious, irresistible, mutiny-inducing trouble." He dipped her dramatically before kissing her again, then righted her and picked up the package.

"Thank you," she said, turning the wrapped book over in her hands. "I didn't get you anything."

"You didn't exactly have advance notice. Next year, though, I expect something spectacular. I know what you can do with this holiday." He ushered her back inside. "Open it."

Bella, now free from the office, launched herself at Jack, who caught her mid-air. "You'll have to meet Mac sometime, Bella. Between the two of you, my apartment may never recover."

Alison pushed up her glasses before unwrapping the gift. Inside was a pristine replica of the Peacock Edition of *Pride and Prejudice*, its teal cover gleaming with gold.

She opened it. Jack's terrible handwriting sprawled across the inscription:

Dear Alison,
"You showed me how insufficient were all my
pretensions to please a woman worthy of being
pleased."
I'm sorry. Can I ask for a rewrite?
– Jack

Alison laughed softly, clutching the book against her chest.

"Jack," she said, "thank you, but I'd much prefer a sequel."

CHAPTER TWENTY-ONE

Two Years Later

Jack

"Are we ready?" Alison asked as she switched on the store register and shooed Mac off the checkout counter for the third time.

"Absolutely, my dearest Isobel." Jack, already in his Captain Drake costume, gave her an extravagant bow. The way she adjusted her blouse and hat—focused, bright, entirely herself—hit him right in the chest.

"Excellent idea wearing the Isobel and Elias costumes for Enemies to Lovers Week," she said, checking her hat in the window's glass before dropping Bella behind the baby gate.

"I'll take any excuse," Jack replied. "Besides, you spent a fortune buying these costumes for us."

"What choice did I have? I'd be devastated if they ever vanished." She disappeared briefly into the office and returned with a wrapped gift. "Speaking of...happy Valentine's Day. I wanted to give you this before customers arrive."

"You got me a hardcover?" Jack set the expertly wrapped book on the counter and pulled out a gleaming silver bookmark tucked into the folds. Its cut-metal pattern was familiar, though he couldn't place it yet. After examining it, he set it aside, peeling the paper carefully—half to admire her technique, half to torture her with anticipation.

Inside was a navy leather-bound copy of *his* book, the one the publisher had released only months before. The hand-tooled cover gleamed softly. Without thinking, he lifted it to his face and inhaled the scent of fresh leather.

His breath caught. "How did you do this?"

"I ordered it ages ago," Alison said, pushing up her glasses. "Then I had a mild panic waiting for the publisher to release the book in time for me to send a copy for rebinding. The bookmark's custom, too. It matches the cover."

Jack picked it up again and saw it—the abstract pattern was pulled straight from his own book cover. Something warm and startling twisted in his chest.

"I can't believe you pulled this off," he murmured. "It's incredible."

"It's your first book," she said simply. "And it's doing great."

He laughed softly, leaning in to kiss her. "You'll find out what it's like soon enough, Ms. I've-Got-An-Agent."

He held her hands then, letting the moment settle. The store hummed with its usual morning sounds: Bella pawing at the baby gate, Mac plotting mischief, the soft whir of the air purifier. It hit him all at once—this life they'd built together, steady and sweet and real.

"I guess it's my turn," he said quietly. "Alison Hughes…I love you. These have been the happiest two years of my life." He reached into his pocket and pulled out a small black velvet box. "Will you please marry me so we can share the rest?"

He opened it. The ring glimmered in the soft shop light.

Alison let out that gasp of hers, the one that had unraveled him the first time he heard it. Her eyes went bright, then brighter, and she let out a breath that shook just a little.

"Yes," she said, almost laughing with joy. "Jack Morrison, I would love to marry you. I can't wait for the next chapter."

THE END

OTHER BOOKS BY
LISA YAROST

Dreamers: A Novel of Coffee, Courtship, and Conspiracy

The man of Emma's dreams has arrived. He's brought trouble, and she can't get him out of her head.

Twenty-two-year-old Emma Morgan feels stuck, still living with her parents while working at JoeStop Coffee Shop, with her handsome best friend Marquel. Then, an odd, quiet customer named Tony invades her dreams. He recruits Emma to help uncover the connection between the decade-long pandemic of people not being able to dream and the pharmaceutical company that sells Slumbera, the condition's only treatment. Emma soon finds herself in the crosshairs when she is noticed by the people who have the most to lose if their scheme is uncovered. Can Emma survive long enough to expose the conspiracy and get Tony out of her head?

Approx. 430 pages

Available in ebook and paperback, exclusively on Amazon.
https://www.amazon.com/dp/B0DM43GNNM

DREAMERS
CHAPTER ONE

Dreamers: A Novel of Coffee, Courtship, and Conspiracy
By Lisa Yarost

FRI, JAN 13, 2034

Dreams have always been precious.

In January 2034, without insurance, they cost $1500 for a thirty day supply. Emma, however, was lucky enough to still have health insurance through her parents at 22, and she dreamed without taking Slumbera.

It was, however, easy to tell her doctor she wasn't dreaming, obtain her REM Deficit Disorder diagnosis, and pick up her prescription for Slumbera for a thirty-dollar copay. It was just as easy to cut the label off the brown prescription bottle with her utility knife and throw it in the trash at work, where nobody would think to dig through the coffee grounds and crumpled napkins to find evidence of her insurance fraud.

Nobody witnessed Emma's criminal activities when she started her 4 am shift at Joe Stop, arriving an hour before Marquel, her best friend and shift partner, was scheduled to start. The streets of Grand Rapids's Eastown neighborhood were deserted.

As she buried the pill label, Emma's phone buzzed. She saw Marquel pressed against the front door, pulling a face like a bug on a windshield, awaiting her. The punk music blaring while she worked had drowned out his knocking.

Snow had settled on his leather motorcycle jacket and his chin-length locs by the time Emma unlocked the door for Marquel, apologizing for making him wait. She stepped aside to make room for his broad frame, bumping elbows in greeting as he passed. Marquel towered over Emma by nearly a foot, and people who knew them sometimes joked about the stark difference between the large dark-skinned man and the pale, scrawny girl he worked with.

"Dang," he said with a grin as she changed the music to the coffee shop's usual mix. "I thought Joe had finally changed the vibe in this joint."

"Nah, just thinking," she replied. The music had been helping her rehash a dream from the night before.

"You're early, Marquel."

"Thought the sidewalks might need clearing. I was right."

"You're a prince. Be sure to log in before you start. Liability."

"Don't worry," he called as he walked toward the back, "I don't work for free."

He returned to the front of the cafe carrying a snow shovel and a bucket of ice melt so heavy that Emma would have had to drag it, managing the weight with such ease that the bucket looked empty in his grasp.

Emma finished setting up, her thoughts returning to her dream. She had been hanging out in an underground punk club, looking fierce in black leather, with pink spiked hair shaved on one side, and sharp eyeliner to match her black lipstick. A man with a buzz cut tapped her on the shoulder and told her to count her fingers, holding up his hands with his fingers splayed, when her alarm went off. The dream somehow sparked a yearning within her to revisit.

Marquel finished the sidewalks, pulling Emma's thoughts back to the present as he joined her behind the counter.

"Marquel, do you want to wake up the espresso machine?"

"My pleasure," he said as he leaned in toward the gleaming Italian monster. "WAKE UUUUP!" he shouted in an impressive heavy metal growl, then mugged and looked for a reaction from the corner of his eye.

"Never gets old," she replied.

After waking the espresso machine for the day, he dialed in the coffee grinders, so each shot took twenty-five seconds to pour. Emma looked on as the smell of fresh coffee filled the shop. It had taken her ages to learn the proper way to adjust the temperamental equipment when she first started working there, but Marquel was a natural, mastering it in less than a week. His movements were deliberate, but not slow. Despite his large hands, he deftly handled the tiny spoons used to adjust the weight of the grounds in the portafilters. Emma chalked this ability up to his guitar skills.

He handed off an espresso shot for her to sample after trying a spoonful for himself and nodded. Inhaling the rich, bitter aroma, Emma closed her eyes as she sipped from the glass. "Mmm. Chocolaty with notes of blueberry and herbs."

"You're full of crap."

"Yeah," she said. "I don't taste any of that. But it's an amazing shot of espresso. It's five-o-clock. You ready?"

"Almost," he said as he grabbed a broken chunk of chalk. "You forgot who's in charge," He wrote her name on the board under the heading of PERSON IN CHARGE, then wiped the dust from his hands. "I don't want to be blamed for this mess."

When Marquel started working at Joe's, Emma tasked him with barista work between rushes while she took orders and ran the register, then switched off when the crush started. His skills surpassed hers, and Emma switched to running the register full time and pitching in when the crowds hit so she wouldn't hinder him. As they prepared for the morning rush, Emma washed the dishes that had collected in the sink while Marquel wiped down tables. Despite enjoying the hot, soapy water, it was murder on her hands during the dry January weather in West Michigan.

While they were still alone, Emma dried her hands and fished in her apron pocket. "Hey," she said as she tossed Marquel the prescription bottle. "Prezzie for ya." At age 27, Marquel couldn't afford health insurance, and he definitely couldn't afford Slumbera.

"Thanks. Sweet dreams," he said as he kissed the bottle and shoved it in his pocket. "What do I owe ya?"

"Don't worry about it." She plunged her hands back into the water. "I'm still living with Mom and Dad, so I have no rent to pay."

At a quarter to seven, Emma took her first break, sitting at an empty corner table and pulling out her phone. Her father messaged a link to a talking dog video on the DeLu app. Emma viewed the video, then closed the app before it gave her a headache. She didn't understand how people spent hours scrolling through video after video, but it seemed like everyone did. After the ban on Chinese-owned Vidly in 2024, American-owned DeLu rose to take its place. The wildly popular short form video app would have ensnared Emma, as well, if not for the headaches it caused her. She tapped a quick reply to her father, then spent the rest of her break grinding through email.

Emma relieved Marquel, who took his break at the same corner table instead of sitting in Joe's messy, windowless office. She brewed fresh coffee, then saw *him*—the man from her dreams—at the register.

Instead of a buzz cut, Finger Guy wore his blond hair in a mid-length e-boy cut, long bangs falling around his thin, clean-shaven face. He'd been in before, but he wasn't a regular.

"How can I help you?" she asked, trying to pull her gaze from his hazel eyes.

Why did I dream about this guy? He's not memorable.

"Double shot cap, please," he said after peering at the menu for a moment. "Name is Tony."

"Thanks, Tony. That will be right up." She took the order sticker from the machine and plastered it onto his cup as she watched him walk to a table.

Well, at least he's not Finger Guy anymore.

Emma occasionally glanced at Tony while she prepared his drink. He was lean, and a few inches taller than she was. His sharp features accentuated the thoughtful pout of his full lips as he watched her work.

"Tony!" she called, placing his drink on the counter.

"Thanks." He took the drink and looked at her bashfully. "See you later." Then he waved, fingers splayed, the same strange way he had in her dream. What she saw barely registered before he was gone, leaving behind only the icy draft from outside when he disappeared through the front door.

Marquel ensured there were no customers present before he spoke. "That was kind of weird. Do you know that guy?"

"I don't think so," she said, taking a drink of water.

"Kind of dorky. Dude was making heart eyes at you, Emma. Maybe you found Mr. Right."

Emma struggled to swallow her water, then started giggling. "We're so mean. He seemed like a nice guy. We don't even know whether Mr. Tony left a tip."

"You mean to tell me a guy that goofy has a chance of being a big tipper? Go home."

"Don't tempt me," she snickered, then regained her professional demeanor when more customers entered the shop. The rush had begun.

Two hours vanished, and it was time for Emma to go to "lunch," if 9:30 could be lunchtime. She returned to the break corner to scarf down a day-old muffin from the FAMILY bin while she read the news, surrounded by the chaotic sounds of customers scrolling through DeLu videos on their phones. The one thing their feeds shared was the irritating, yet pervasive, Slumbera ad. Its jingle, an old song called "Dream a Little Dream of Me," was something Emma would pay money never to hear again. She rested, eyes closed, head tipped back against the wall.

Marquel nudged her arm to wake her. "Hey. Wanna break me?"

Emma opened her eyes halfway. "For waking me? Yes. I. Will. Break. You." She took a deep breath and shook her head. "How long was I out?"

"Not long, maybe ten minutes. Nobody noticed, except for that drool dripping down your face."

She wiped her mouth, finding it dry. "Cute. Thanks. Take your break."

He removed his apron and ducked out the front door without his coat, striding toward Past Prose Used Books, which opened at ten. It had stopped snowing, but Emma could tell it was still frigid outside by the way Marquel's breath trailed in a cloud behind him.

Joe entered the store from the back door a few minutes later, clapping his gloved hands and rubbing them together. "Good morning!"

"How are you, Joe?"

"Cold. I'm very, very cold." He shoved his gloves in his pockets and poured a cup of drip coffee for himself. "Well, I'll be in my office if you need me. Thanks for clearing the sidewalks."

"Thank Marquel. I stayed in where it's warm."

"Will do." Joe gave her a little two-finger salute, his face wrinkling as he smiled and closed himself in the back.

Marquel returned five minutes before the end of his meal break, paper bag in hand.

"Ooh, treasure!" Emma said. "What did you get?"

"Dan bought a bunch of vintage horror from an estate. They're in rough shape, but they'll still read fine." He set the bag on the counter and grabbed his apron.

"Can I see?" Emma peeked into the bag.

"Well, since you're already pawing through it, help yourself."

She pulled four tattered paperbacks from the bag to admire their glorious, tawdry eighties covers.

"Don't breathe on these things too hard, Marquel. They'll disintegrate."

"I know, right? You want them when I'm done?"

"They're pretty fragile. What if I ruin them?"

"I bought them to read, not to collect. If they last through both of us I'll trade them in to Dan for more credit. If they don't?" He shrugged.

"Then yes, please.

Instead of going to her car after her shift, Emma rushed out the front door and into the used bookstore, an old-fashioned bell announcing her arrival. Dan, seated next to the register, peeked around a haphazard pile of books. "Hey, Girl! Anything new?"

"No, but I hear you have some new stuff." Books spilled from every shelf in Past Prose, creating a chaotic yet comforting scene. Emma wondered how Dan could fit even one more book into the already overflowing space.

"New to me, anyway." He gestured to the towering stack of well-worn paperbacks, their spines cracked and faded, crowding the counter. "Marquel mentioned they were all Reading Copies, right?"

"Right." Tilting her head to read the cracked spines, Emma found a few that she hadn't seen before. As she sorted through them, she noted Dan hadn't exaggerated their condition: these had all seen hard usage. A dollar each made them a steal, despite lacking collector value.

Emma chose five books from the stack. As she reached for her wallet, Dan protested. "You expect me to take your money after you cleared my sidewalk this morning? Put that away."

"No dice," she replied, taking out some cash. "Marquel shoveled the sidewalks. I just watched like the bum I am."

"Then give that money to him. I don't want it," he insisted, waving it away. "And tell him thanks. I wasn't looking forward to doing that today."

"I'll do that," she said as Dan bagged her books. "How is the used book business, anyway?"

"Terrible," he confided. "I started this shop forty years ago, and it's like owning your job, but I own the entire building, so the rent makes up for it."

"Wait, you own Joe's space?"

He nodded. "And the salon's space on the other side of this store."

"What's upstairs?" Each shop featured a second story.

"Above this store? My apartment. The other ones are storage. They're apartments, too, but I haven't rented them out in years."

Emma's stomach jumped. "Have you thought about it?"

"They're pretty outdated."

"You mean they have *vintage charm*?" she asked.

"Are you telling me you want to live in a one hundred thirty-year-old apartment that smells like coffee?"

She raised an eyebrow. "Maybe?"

Dan reached under the counter, pulled out a massive keyring and held it up by one of the keys. "If you want to take a look, you can. Outside door next to this one, the unit above the coffee shop. The other one is my place. Be careful walking around in there. Like I said, it's storage right now."

Emma's eyes widened as she grabbed the key. The idea of having her own place was enticing, if unrealistic. She had no idea what Dan would charge. Regardless, she wouldn't pass on a chance to poke around an old building unsupervised.

She walked upstairs and fumbled with the heavy keyring to unlock the apartment door, its neglected hinges groaning as it opened. While the cafe didn't feel large, the apartment above it felt enormous. The bright space overlooking the street smelled of cold, stale air and coffee. Dirty windows, their wooden frames covered with peeling white paint, filled the spacious living room with natural light.

Emma wove through old furniture and piles of boxes, careful not to disturb the thick layer of dust that coated everything. The kitchen, equipped with white steel cabinets and laminate countertops, lay to her left. Opposite was a laminate and steel dining table with matching chairs in the dinette, perhaps left by a previous tenant.

Towards the back was the pink-and-black-tiled bathroom, facing a small bedroom on the right, while a large bedroom featuring a window and an exterior door comprised the back of the apartment. From the doorway, Emma saw the cafe's rear roof and a metal stairway leading to the parking area. It had a patio! Dusty boxes, furniture, and uneven walls filled every room.

Emma was in love.

She photographed the whole place on her way out and returned Dan's keys.

"It's a nightmare, isn't it? I tried to warn you," he said as he took them back.

"I kind of liked it. How much would you consider charging for it?"

"I don't know," he said reluctantly. "How would I clear everything out of it?"

"What's in the boxes?"

"Books," he said quietly.

"Oh, my," she murmured after a moment. "Personal?"

"No. They were meant to be stock."

"So, what's in the third apartment?"

"More boxes."

"Of books?"

"Of books," he said, leveling his gaze at her. "I told you it's a terrible business."

When Emma came home to an empty house, she dropped the bag of books on her dresser, determined to use the opportunity to take a power nap after a long work week. She closed her blackout curtains and crawled onto the bed, falling asleep the moment she settled into her pillow, then woke with a start at the sound of the kitchen door. Emma stumbled into the hallway, checking her phone to discover she had been asleep for three hours. Her mother stood in the darkened kitchen, her hand on the granite countertop, looking disappointed, as usual.

"Hey, Mom." Emma drowsily ran her fingers through her hair. "How was work?"

"It's past five, Emma. Weren't you going to start dinner?"

"Didn't Dad tell you he was picking up pizza?"

"You two never tell me what you have planned." Frustration gnawed around the edges of her voice. "Did you dust and vacuum?"

"I was planning to do it tomorrow. It's my day off."

"It's my day off, too. I was hoping not to have to listen to the vacuum."

"Are we really talking about the vacuum here?" Emma asked, squinting.

"Honey, I just — I don't know what you're doing." Her mother hung her purse near the door.

Emma, still groggy, did her best to appease her mother. "I was napping. I didn't mean to sleep this long."

"That's not what I meant. You're a bright young woman who's working in a coffee shop when you should be in school. We would help you."

"What would I study? You're a lawyer, like you always wanted to be. Dad's a chemist, like he always wanted to be. What if I go through school, only to discover that I chose to study the wrong thing? I don't even know what I'm good at, besides running Joe's."

"That's not a forever job, Emma."

"Maybe not, but it's the job I have right now, and I do it well. Let me be good at something for a while, okay?"

Her mother sighed, trudging toward her bedroom. "We'll talk more about this later."

I'm sure we will, Mom.

While her mother slammed drawers and doors in the bedroom, changing from her office clothes with exaggerated sighs, Emma set the table with paper plates and napkins, the traditional tableware for pizza, pouring iced tea for three.

Her father's arrival defused the situation, as always, filling the house with the welcome aroma of pepperoni pizza and cheesy bread. There was little conversation as they each devoured their dinner, with Emma trying her best not to wince at her mother's habit of soaking up the grease from each slice with a paper towel and a sigh, and meticulously picking the pepperoni from each slice to hand to her father.

Why doesn't she just get her own cheese pizza instead of making a show of it all?

After dinner, Emma chose a random book from the pile beside her, losing herself in the paperback until she could barely keep her eyes open. She surveyed her childhood bedroom, equipped with the same white bedroom set, worn student desk, and bookcase she had used since the age of twelve, then flipped through her apartment photos again.

It's full, but it isn't hoarder full. Even if I could afford it, how would I empty it out?

With a sigh and a frown, she turned off the lights, deciding to sleep on it for the night.

Emma walked between the shelves, her steps muffled by walls of books, each shelving unit as tall as she could reach. Lost in thought, she trailed a hand along the bookshelves as she walked, trying to recall what she was looking for.

"Hey," said a quiet voice behind her. With a start, she turned and saw Tony.

"Hey," she replied, narrowing her eyes at the stranger following her.

"Can you do me a favor?" He didn't wait for a response. Instead, he instructed, "Count your fingers."

Emma noted with amazement that each hand had seven fingers. "Am I dreaming?"

"Yeah," he muttered, sweeping his bangs to the side. "Now we can talk."

"Are you a dream? I'm so confused."

"Sort of. I'm not your dream, but I'm in your dream."

"How? Why?" She scowled at him. "How long have you been creeping on my dreams?"

"It's not like that," Tony said. "I am not creeping on you. You've met me both times I've been here, I promise. Listen: this is complicated, but you'll understand in time. What you need to know now is that we're both Dreamers. There are a lot of us out there, but it's hard to find each other."

"I suppose so, if you're reduced to invading each other's minds," she muttered, unable to escape the creepers even in her dreams. "It's like using someone's Wi-Fi without their permission. Can I set a password?"

"I'm sorry," he replied, his patience waning, "but this isn't for nothing. Did you ever wonder what caused REM Deficit Disorder and why so many people suffer from it?"

"Hasn't everyone? There are a lot of people way smarter than I am working on that problem, and they haven't found the answers yet. Do you really think a barista can figure it out because I'm a Dreamer? That doesn't make me a superhero. It makes me lucky." She shook her head. "And why do you have to hack my dreams in order to talk about this? You could walk into the cafe."

"Because RDD didn't just happen, Emma. It was made."

"What kind of conspiracy garbage is this? RDD isn't some super virus. It's like depression. Nobody *made* depression."

Tony glared at the corner behind her and sighed. "But depression didn't appear out of nowhere; RDD did."

"This is nuts, and if this," Emma waved her hands wildly, encompassing the entire dream, "is real, you've found a way to creep on other people's dreams. But it isn't real, so I'm getting worked up over nothing."

"Okay, two things. One, I will prove next week that this is real. Two, I have a question for you. Does anyone have something to gain from RDD? Think about that." He rounded the bookshelves, prompting Emma to follow him. Reaching the end of the aisle, she found he had vanished. Once more, she was alone in her dream.